FARMHOUSE COOKING

Comforting, simple & delicious dishes
made with the freshest ingredients

pil

Publications International, Ltd.

Photographs on front cover and pages 3, 34, 64, 96, 126, 156 and 161 © Shutterstock.com. All other photographs and all recipes © Publications International, Ltd.

Pictured on the front cover: Blueberry Apple Skillet Crumble *(page 160)*.

Pictured on the back cover *(clockwise from top right):* Raisin-Nut Oatmeal *(page 14),* Forty-Clove Chicken Filice *(page 86),* Sausage Rice Soup *(page 36)* and Asparagus and Arugula Salad *(page 134)*.

ISBN: 978-1-64030-637-0

Manufactured in China.

8 7 6 5 4 3 2 1

Microwave Cooking: Microwave ovens vary in wattage. Use the cooking times as guidelines and check for doneness before adding more time.

CONTENTS

BREAKFAST

APPLE BUTTER SPICE MUFFINS

MAKES 12 MUFFINS

½ cup sugar

1 teaspoon ground cinnamon

¼ teaspoon ground nutmeg

⅛ teaspoon ground allspice

½ cup pecans or walnuts, chopped

2 cups all-purpose flour

2 teaspoons baking powder

¼ teaspoon salt

1 cup milk

¼ cup vegetable oil

1 egg

¼ cup apple butter

1. Preheat oven to 400°F. Line 12 standard (2½-inch) muffin cups with paper baking cups.

2. Combine sugar, cinnamon, nutmeg and allspice in large bowl. Remove 2 tablespoons sugar mixture to small bowl; toss with pecans until coated. Add flour, baking powder and salt to remaining sugar mixture.

3. Whisk milk, oil and egg in medium bowl until well blended. Add to flour mixture; stir just until moistened. Spoon 1 tablespoon batter into each prepared muffin cup. Top with 1 teaspoon apple butter. Spoon remaining batter evenly over apple butter; sprinkle with pecan mixture.

4. Bake 20 to 25 minutes or until golden brown and toothpick inserted into centers comes out clean. Remove to wire rack to cool 10 minutes. Serve warm or cool completely.

ZUCCHINI-TOMATO FRITTATA

MAKES 4 SERVINGS

1 tablespoon olive oil

1 cup sliced zucchini

1 cup broccoli florets

1 cup diced red or yellow bell pepper

6 eggs, lightly beaten

½ cup cottage cheese

½ cup rehydrated sun-dried tomatoes (1 ounce dry), coarsely chopped*

¼ cup chopped green onions

¼ cup chopped fresh basil

⅛ teaspoon ground red pepper

2 tablespoons shredded Parmesan cheese

Paprika (optional)

To rehydrate sun-dried tomatoes, pour 1 cup boiling water over tomatoes in small bowl. Let stand 5 to 10 minutes or until softened; drain well.

1. Preheat broiler. Heat oil in 10-inch ovenproof skillet over high heat. Add zucchini, broccoli and bell pepper; cook and stir 3 to 4 minutes or until vegetables are crisp-tender.

2. Whisk eggs, cottage cheese, sun-dried tomatoes, green onions, basil and ground red pepper in medium bowl until well blended. Pour egg mixture over vegetables in skillet. Cook, uncovered, gently lifting sides of frittata so uncooked egg flows underneath. Cook 7 to 8 minutes or until frittata is almost set and golden brown on bottom. Sprinkle with cheese.

3. Broil about 5 inches from heat 3 to 5 minutes or until top is golden brown. Sprinkle with paprika, if desired. Serve immediately.

CORNMEAL PANCAKES

MAKES 4 SERVINGS

1½ cups yellow cornmeal

¾ cup all-purpose flour

1½ teaspoons baking powder

1 teaspoon salt

1⅓ cups plain Greek yogurt

⅔ cup milk

2 eggs, lightly beaten

¼ cup sugar

2 tablespoons plus
2 teaspoons butter,
melted, divided

Fresh blueberries (optional)

Maple syrup (optional)

1. Combine cornmeal, flour, baking powder and salt in medium bowl; mix well. Whisk yogurt, milk, eggs, sugar and 2 tablespoons butter in large bowl until well blended. Stir in cornmeal mixture; let stand 5 minutes.

2. Brush griddle or large skillet with 1 teaspoon butter; heat over medium heat. Drop batter by ⅓ cupfuls onto griddle. Cook 3 minutes or until tops of pancakes are bubbly and appear dry. Turn and cook 2 minutes or until bottoms are golden brown, adding remaining 1 teaspoon butter as needed. Serve with blueberries and maple syrup, if desired.

GLAZED CINNAMON COFFEECAKE

MAKES 6 TO 8 SERVINGS

STREUSEL

- ¼ cup biscuit baking mix
- ¼ cup packed brown sugar
- ½ teaspoon ground cinnamon

BATTER

- 1½ cups biscuit baking mix
- ¾ cup granulated sugar
- ½ cup vanilla or plain yogurt
- 1 egg, lightly beaten
- 1 teaspoon vanilla

GLAZE

- 1 to 2 tablespoons milk
- 1 cup powdered sugar
- ½ cup sliced almonds (optional)

SLOW COOKER DIRECTIONS

1. Generously coat 4-quart round slow cooker with butter or spray with nonstick cooking spray. Cut parchment paper to fit bottom of stoneware and press into place. Spray paper lightly with cooking spray.

2. For streusel, combine ¼ cup baking mix, brown sugar and cinnamon in small bowl; mix well.

3. For batter, combine 1½ cups baking mix, granulated sugar, yogurt, egg and vanilla in medium bowl; mix well. Spread half of batter in slow cooker; sprinkle with half of streusel. Repeat layers.

4. Line lid of slow cooker with two paper towels. Cover; cook on HIGH 1¾ to 2 hours or until toothpick inserted into center comes out clean and cake springs back when gently pressed. Turn off heat. Let cake stand, uncovered, 10 minutes. Invert onto plate; peel off parchment paper. Invert again onto serving plate.

5. For glaze, whisk milk into powdered sugar in small bowl, 1 tablespoon at a time, until desired consistency is reached. Spoon glaze over top of cake. Sprinkle with almonds, if desired.

RAISIN-NUT OATMEAL

MAKES 4 SERVINGS

3¾ cups water

2⅔ cups old-fashioned oats

⅔ cup raisins

½ cup sliced almonds, toasted*

⅓ cup nonfat dry milk powder

⅓ cup packed brown sugar

½ teaspoon salt

½ teaspoon ground cinnamon

⅛ teaspoon ground ginger

To toast almonds, spread in single layer on baking sheet. Bake in preheated 350°F oven 5 minutes or until golden brown, stirring frequently.

1. Bring water to a boil in large saucepan over high heat. Stir in oats, raisins, almonds, dry milk powder, brown sugar, salt, cinnamon and ginger until well blended.

2. Reduce heat to medium; cook and stir 4 to 5 minutes or until thick and creamy.

VARIATIONS: To add extra flavor to your oatmeal, toast the oats first: Cook and stir the oats in 1 tablespoon butter over medium heat about 4 minutes or until the oats are browned and fragrant. Try adding fresh or roasted fruit for toppings, or you can even use frozen fruit—stir it in at the beginning of the cooking time and it will thaw by the time the oatmeal is ready. For a protein boost, swirl in your favorite nut butter at the end of the cooking time. Or top with a spoonful of yogurt or ricotta cheese.

SAWMILL BISCUITS AND GRAVY

MAKES 8 SERVINGS

3 tablespoons canola or vegetable oil, divided

8 ounces bulk breakfast sausage

2¼ cups plus 3 tablespoons biscuit baking mix, divided

2⅔ cups whole milk, divided

¼ teaspoon salt

¼ teaspoon black pepper

1. Preheat oven to 450°F. Heat 1 tablespoon oil in large skillet over medium heat. Add sausage; cook and stir 6 to 8 minutes or until browned, stirring to break up meat. Remove to plate with slotted spoon.

2. Add remaining 2 tablespoons oil to skillet. Add 3 tablespoons biscuit mix; whisk until smooth. Gradually add 2 cups milk; cook and stir 3 to 4 minutes or until mixture comes to a boil. Cook and stir 1 minute or until thickened. Add sausage and any juices; cook and stir 2 minutes. Season with salt and pepper.

3. Combine remaining 2¼ cups biscuit mix and ⅔ cup milk in medium bowl; stir until blended. Spoon batter into eight mounds on gravy mixture in skillet.

4. Bake 8 to 10 minutes or until golden. Serve warm.

RASPBERRY CORN MUFFINS

MAKES 12 MUFFINS

1 cup all-purpose flour

¾ cup yellow cornmeal

½ cup sugar

2 teaspoons baking powder

½ teaspoon baking soda

½ teaspoon salt

⅔ cup plain Greek yogurt

⅓ cup milk

¼ cup (½ stick) butter, melted

1 egg

1¼ cups fresh or frozen raspberries

1. Preheat oven to 400°F. Line 12 standard (2½-inch) muffin cups with paper baking cups.

2. Combine flour, cornmeal, sugar, baking powder, baking soda and salt in large bowl; mix well. Whisk yogurt, milk, butter and egg in medium bowl until well blended. Add to flour mixture; stir just until dry ingredients are moistened. *Do not overmix.* Gently fold in raspberries. Spoon batter evenly into prepared cups.

3. Bake 16 to 18 minutes or until toothpick inserted into centers comes out clean. Cool in pan 5 minutes; remove to wire rack to cool completely.

MAPLE PECAN GRANOLA

MAKES ABOUT 6 CUPS

6 tablespoons vegetable oil

¼ cup maple syrup

¼ cup packed dark brown sugar

1½ teaspoons vanilla

½ teaspoon ground cinnamon

½ teaspoon coarse salt

3 cups old-fashioned rolled oats

1½ cups pecans, coarsely chopped

¾ cup shredded coconut

¼ cup ground flax seeds

¼ cup water

Plain yogurt or milk (optional)

1. Preheat oven to 350°F. Line large rimmed baking sheet with parchment paper.

2. Whisk oil, maple syrup, brown sugar, vanilla, cinnamon and salt in large bowl until blended. Add oats, pecans, coconut and flax seeds; stir until evenly coated. Stir in water. Spread mixture on prepared baking sheet, pressing into even layer.

3. Bake 30 minutes or until granola is golden brown and fragrant. Cool completely on baking sheet. Serve with yogurt or milk, if desired. Store leftovers in an airtight container at room temperature up to 1 month.

NOTE: For chunky granola, do not stir during baking. For loose granola, stir every 10 minutes during baking.

CINNAMON FRENCH TOAST CASSEROLE
MAKES 6 TO 8 SERVINGS

1 large loaf French bread, cut into 1½-inch slices

3½ cups milk

9 eggs

1½ cups granulated sugar, divided

1 tablespoon vanilla

½ teaspoon salt

6 to 8 baking apples, such as McIntosh or Cortland, peeled and sliced

1 teaspoon ground cinnamon

½ teaspoon ground nutmeg

Powdered sugar (optional)

1. Spray 13×9-inch baking dish with nonstick cooking spray. Arrange bread slices in single layer in prepared dish.

2. Whisk milk, eggs, 1 cup granulated sugar, vanilla and salt in large bowl until well blended. Pour half of egg mixture over bread. Layer apple slices over bread. Pour remaining half of egg mixture over apples.

3. Combine remaining ½ cup granulated sugar, cinnamon and nutmeg in small bowl; sprinkle over casserole. Cover and refrigerate overnight.

4. Preheat oven to 350°F. Bake, uncovered, 1 hour or until set. Sprinkle with powdered sugar, if desired.

CHEDDAR BISCUITS

MAKES 15 BISCUITS

2 cups all-purpose flour

1 tablespoon sugar

1 tablespoon baking powder

2¼ teaspoons garlic powder, divided

¾ teaspoon plus pinch of salt, divided

1 cup whole milk

½ cup (1 stick) plus 3 tablespoons butter, melted, divided

2 cups (8 ounces) shredded Cheddar cheese

½ teaspoon dried parsley flakes

1. Preheat oven to 450°F. Line large baking sheet with parchment paper.

2. Combine flour, sugar, baking powder, 2 teaspoons garlic powder and ¾ teaspoon salt in large bowl; mix well. Add milk and ½ cup melted butter; stir just until dry ingredients are moistened. Stir in cheese just until blended. Drop scant ¼ cupfuls of dough about 1½ inches apart onto prepared baking sheet.

3. Bake 10 to 12 minutes or until golden brown. Meanwhile, combine remaining 3 tablespoons melted butter, ¼ teaspoon garlic powder, pinch of salt and parsley flakes in small bowl; brush over biscuits immediately after removing from oven. Serve warm.

STRAWBERRY-TOPPED PANCAKES

MAKES 4 SERVINGS (12 LARGE PANCAKES)

3 cups sliced fresh strawberries

¼ cup seedless strawberry jam

2½ cups all-purpose flour

½ cup sugar

2 teaspoons baking powder

2 teaspoons baking soda

½ teaspoon salt

2½ cups buttermilk

2 eggs, lightly beaten

2 tablespoons vegetable oil

Whipped cream (optional)

1. Combine strawberries and strawberry jam in medium bowl; stir gently to coat. Set aside while preparing pancakes.

2. Combine flour, sugar, baking powder, baking soda and salt in large bowl; mix well. Add buttermilk and eggs; whisk until blended.

3. Heat 1 tablespoon oil in large skillet over medium heat or brush griddle with oil. For each pancake, pour ½ cup of batter into skillet, spreading into 5- to 6-inch circle. Cook 3 to 4 minutes or until bottom is golden brown and small bubbles appear on surface. Turn pancake; cook 2 minutes or until golden brown. Add additional oil to skillet as needed.

4. For each serving, stack three pancakes; top with strawberry mixture. Garnish with whipped cream.

BACON AND POTATO QUICHE

MAKES 8 SERVINGS

1 refrigerated pie crust (half of 15-ounce package)

12 ounces thick-cut bacon, cut crosswise into ½-inch pieces

½ medium onion, chopped

½ pound Yukon Gold potatoes, peeled and cut into ¼-inch dice

½ teaspoon chopped fresh thyme

1½ cups half-and-half

4 eggs

½ teaspoon salt

½ teaspoon black pepper

¾ cup (3 ounces) shredded Swiss or white Cheddar cheese

2 tablespoons chopped fresh chives

1. Preheat oven to 450°F. Line baking sheet with foil.

2. Roll out pie crust into 12-inch circle on floured surface. Line 9-inch pie plate with crust, pressing firmly against bottom and up side of plate. Trim crust to leave 1-inch overhang; fold under and flute edge. Prick bottom of crust with fork. Bake about 8 minutes or until lightly browned. Remove to wire rack to cool slightly. *Reduce oven temperature to 375°F.*

3. Cook bacon in large skillet over medium heat about 10 minutes or until crisp, stirring occasionally. Drain on paper towel-lined plate. Drain all but 1 tablespoon drippings from skillet. Add onion, potatoes and thyme to skillet; cook about 10 minutes or until vegetables are tender, stirring occasionally.

4. Place pie plate on prepared baking sheet. Whisk half-and-half, eggs, salt and pepper in medium bowl until well blended. Sprinkle cheese evenly over bottom of crust; top with vegetable mixture. Pour in egg mixture; sprinkle with chives.

5. Bake 35 to 40 minutes or until quiche is set and knife inserted into center comes out clean. Let stand 10 minutes before slicing.

APPLE RING COFFEECAKE

MAKES 12 SERVINGS

3 cups all-purpose flour

1 teaspoon baking soda

1 teaspoon salt

1 teaspoon ground cinnamon

1 cup chopped walnuts

1½ cups granulated sugar

1 cup vegetable oil

2 eggs

2 teaspoons vanilla

2 medium tart apples, peeled, cored and chopped

Powdered sugar (optional)

1. Preheat oven to 325°F. Grease 10-inch tube pan.

2. Sift flour, baking soda, salt and cinnamon into large bowl. Stir in walnuts until blended.

3. Combine granulated sugar, oil, eggs and vanilla in medium bowl; mix well. Stir in apples. Stir into flour mixture just until moistened. Spoon batter into prepared pan; smooth top.

4. Bake 1 hour or until toothpick inserted near center comes out clean. Cool cake in pan 10 minutes. Loosen edges with metal spatula, if necessary. Remove to wire rack to cool completely. Sprinkle with powdered sugar, if desired, just before serving.

SAUSAGE SKILLET BREAKFAST

MAKES 4 SERVINGS

1½ pounds red potatoes

3 uncooked sausage links (about 4 ounces each), cut into ¼-inch slices

2 tablespoons butter

1½ teaspoons caraway seeds

4 cups shredded red cabbage

1. Cut potatoes into ¼- to ½-inch pieces. Place in microwavable baking dish. Cover and microwave on HIGH 3 minutes. Stir potatoes; microwave 2 minutes or just until tender.

2. Cook sausage in large skillet over medium-high heat 8 minutes or until browned and cooked through, stirring occasionally. Remove to paper towel-lined plate. Drain off drippings.

3. Melt butter in same skillet. Add potatoes and caraway seeds; cook 6 to 8 minutes or until potatoes are golden brown and tender, stirring occasionally.

4. Return sausage to skillet; stir in cabbage. Cover and cook 3 minutes or until cabbage is slightly wilted. Uncover; cook and stir 3 to 4 minutes or just until cabbage is tender.

SOUPS & STEWS

SAUSAGE RICE SOUP

MAKES 4 TO 6 SERVINGS

2 teaspoons olive oil

8 ounces Italian sausage, casings removed

1 small onion, chopped

½ teaspoon fennel seeds

1 tablespoon tomato paste

4 cups chicken broth

1 can (about 14 ounces) whole peeled tomatoes, undrained, tomatoes crushed with hands or chopped

1½ cups water

½ cup uncooked rice

¼ teaspoon salt

⅛ teaspoon black pepper

2 to 3 ounces baby spinach

⅓ cup shredded mozzarella cheese (optional)

1. Heat oil in large saucepan or Dutch oven over medium-high heat. Add sausage; cook about 8 minutes or until browned, breaking up meat into bite-sized pieces. Add onion; cook and stir 5 minutes or until softened. Add fennel seeds; cook and stir 30 seconds. Add tomato paste; cook and stir 1 minute.

2. Stir in broth, tomatoes with juice, water, rice, salt and pepper; bring to a boil. Reduce heat to medium-low; cook about 18 minutes or until rice is tender. Stir in spinach; cook about 3 minutes or until wilted. Season with additional salt and pepper.

3. Sprinkle with cheese, if desired, just before serving.

CHICKEN AND HERB STEW

MAKES 4 SERVINGS

½ cup all-purpose flour

½ teaspoon salt

¼ teaspoon black pepper

¼ teaspoon paprika

4 chicken drumsticks

4 chicken thighs

2 tablespoons olive oil

12 ounces new potatoes, quartered

2 carrots, quartered lengthwise, then cut crosswise into 3-inch pieces

1 green bell pepper, cut into thin strips

¾ cup chopped onion

2 cloves garlic, minced

1¾ cups water

¼ cup dry white wine

2 cubes chicken bouillon

1 tablespoon chopped fresh oregano

1 teaspoon chopped fresh rosemary leaves

2 tablespoons chopped fresh Italian parsley

1. Combine flour, salt, black pepper and paprika in shallow dish; mix well. Coat chicken with flour mixture; shake off excess.

2. Heat oil in large skillet over medium-high heat. Add chicken; cook about 5 minutes per side or until browned. Remove to plate.

3. Add potatoes, carrots, bell pepper, onion and garlic to same skillet; cook and stir 6 minutes or until vegetables are lightly browned. Add water, wine and bouillon; cook 1 minute, scraping up browned bits from bottom of skillet. Stir in oregano and rosemary.

4. Place chicken on top of vegetable mixture, turning several times to coat. Cover and cook 45 to 50 minutes or until chicken is cooked through (165°F), turning occasionally. Sprinkle with parsley.

BAKED POTATO SOUP

MAKES 6 TO 8 SERVINGS

3 medium russet potatoes
(about 1 pound)

¼ cup (½ stick) butter

1 cup chopped onion

½ cup all-purpose flour

4 cups chicken or vegetable
broth

1½ cups instant mashed
potato flakes

1 cup water

1 cup half-and-half

1 teaspoon salt

½ teaspoon dried basil

½ teaspoon dried thyme

¼ teaspoon black pepper

1 cup (4 ounces) shredded
Cheddar cheese

4 slices bacon, crisp-cooked
and crumbled

1 green onion, chopped

1. Preheat oven to 400°F. Scrub potatoes and prick in several places with fork. Place in baking pan; bake 1 hour. Cool completely; peel and cut into ½-inch pieces. (Potatoes can be prepared several days in advance; refrigerate until ready to use.)

2. Melt butter in large saucepan or Dutch oven over medium heat. Add onion; cook and stir 3 minutes or until softened. Whisk in flour; cook and stir 1 minute. Gradually whisk in broth until well blended. Stir in mashed potato flakes, water, half-and-half, salt, basil, thyme and pepper; bring to a boil over medium-high heat. Reduce heat to medium; cook 5 minutes.

3. Stir in baked potato cubes; cook 10 to 15 minutes or until soup is thickened and heated through. Top with cheese, bacon and green onion.

MINESTRONE SOUP

MAKES 4 TO 6 SERVINGS

1 tablespoon olive oil

½ cup chopped onion

1 stalk celery, diced

1 carrot, diced

2 cloves garlic, minced

2 cups vegetable broth

1½ cups water

1 bay leaf

¾ teaspoon salt

½ teaspoon dried basil

½ teaspoon dried oregano

¼ teaspoon dried thyme

¼ teaspoon sugar

Ground black pepper

1 can (about 15 ounces) dark red kidney beans, rinsed and drained

1 can (about 15 ounces) navy beans or cannellini beans, rinsed and drained

1 can (about 14 ounces) diced tomatoes

1 cup diced zucchini (about 1 small)

½ cup uncooked small shell pasta

½ cup frozen cut green beans

¼ cup dry red wine

1 cup packed chopped fresh spinach

Grated Parmesan cheese (optional)

1. Heat oil in large saucepan or Dutch oven over medium-high heat. Add onion, celery, carrot and garlic; cook and stir 5 to 7 minutes or until vegetables are tender. Add broth, water, bay leaf, salt, basil, oregano, thyme, sugar and pepper; bring to a boil.

2. Stir in kidney beans, navy beans, tomatoes, zucchini, pasta, green beans and wine; cook 10 minutes, stirring occasionally.

3. Add spinach; cook 2 minutes or until pasta and zucchini are tender. Remove and discard bay leaf. Ladle into bowls; serve with cheese, if desired.

CHICKEN, BARLEY AND VEGETABLE SOUP

MAKES 6 SERVINGS

8 ounces boneless skinless chicken breasts, cut into ½-inch pieces

8 ounces boneless skinless chicken thighs, cut into ½-inch pieces

¾ teaspoon salt

¼ teaspoon black pepper

1 tablespoon olive oil

½ cup uncooked pearl barley

4 cans (about 14 ounces each) chicken broth

2 cups water

1 bay leaf

2 cups whole baby carrots

2 cups diced peeled potatoes

2 cups sliced mushrooms

2 cups frozen peas

3 tablespoons sour cream

1 tablespoon chopped fresh dill *or* 1 teaspoon dried dill weed

1. Sprinkle chicken with salt and pepper. Heat oil in Dutch oven or large saucepan over medium-high heat. Add chicken; cook without stirring 2 minutes or until golden brown. Turn chicken; cook 2 minutes. Remove to plate.

2. Add barley to Dutch oven; cook and stir 1 to 2 minutes or until barley begins to brown, adding 1 tablespoon broth if needed to prevent burning. Add remaining broth, water and bay leaf; bring to a boil. Reduce heat to low; cover and cook 30 minutes.

3. Add chicken, carrots, potatoes and mushrooms; cook 10 minutes or until vegetables are tender, stirring occasionally. Add peas; cook 2 minutes. Remove and discard bay leaf.

4. Top soup with sour cream and dill. Serve immediately.

SPLIT PEA SOUP

MAKES 6 SERVINGS

1 package (16 ounces) dried green or yellow split peas

7 cups water

1 pound smoked ham hocks *or* 4 ounces smoked sausage links, quartered and sliced

2 carrots, chopped

1 onion, chopped

¾ teaspoon salt

½ teaspoon dried basil

¼ teaspoon dried oregano

¼ teaspoon black pepper

1. Rinse split peas in colander under cold running water; discard any debris or blemished peas.

2. Combine split peas, water, ham hocks, carrots, onion, salt, basil, oregano and pepper in large saucepan or Dutch oven; bring to a boil over high heat. Reduce heat to medium-low; cook 1 hour and 15 minutes or until peas are tender, stirring occasionally. Stir frequently near end of cooking to prevent soup from scorching.

3. Remove ham hocks to plate; let stand until cool enough to handle. Remove ham from hocks; chop meat and discard bones.

4. Place 3 cups soup in blender or food processor; blend until smooth. (Or use hand-held immersion blender to partially blend soup in saucepan.) Return blended soup to saucepan; stir in ham. If soup is too thick, add water until desired consistency is reached. Cook just until heated through.

CHICKEN NOODLE SOUP

MAKES 8 SERVINGS

2 tablespoons butter

1 cup chopped onion

1 cup sliced carrots

½ cup diced celery

2 tablespoons vegetable oil

1 pound chicken breast tenderloins

1 pound chicken thigh fillets

4 cups chicken broth, divided

2 cups water

1 tablespoon minced fresh parsley, plus additional for garnish

1½ teaspoons salt

½ teaspoon black pepper

3 cups uncooked egg noodles

1. Melt butter in large saucepan or Dutch oven over medium-low heat. Add onion, carrots and celery; cook 15 minutes or until vegetables are soft, stirring occasionally.

2. Meanwhile, heat oil in large skillet over medium-high heat. Add chicken in single layer; cook about 6 minutes per side or until lightly browned and cooked through. Remove to cutting board.

3. Add 1 cup broth to skillet; cook 1 minute, scraping up any browned bits from bottom of skillet. Add broth to vegetables in saucepan. Stir in remaining 3 cups broth, water, 1 tablespoon parsley, salt and pepper.

4. Chop chicken into 1-inch pieces when cool enough to handle. Add to soup; bring to a boil over medium-high heat. Reduce heat to medium-low; cook 15 minutes. Add noodles; cook 15 minutes or until noodles are tender. Garnish with additional parsley.

OLD-FASHIONED BEEF STEW

MAKES 6 SERVINGS

2 tablespoons olive oil, divided

1½ pounds boneless beef top or bottom round steak, trimmed and cut into 1-inch pieces

4 cups sliced mushrooms

2 cloves garlic, minced

2 cups baby carrots

2 cups beef broth

2 tablespoons tomato paste

¾ teaspoon dried thyme

½ teaspoon salt

½ teaspoon black pepper

2 bay leaves

2 medium onions, cut into wedges

2 cups frozen cut green beans

3 tablespoons water

3 tablespoons all-purpose flour

1. Heat 1 tablespoon oil in Dutch oven over medium-high heat. Cook beef in two batches until browned; remove to plate.

2. Heat remaining 1 tablespoon oil in Dutch oven. Add mushrooms; cook about 8 minutes or until browned. Add garlic; cook and stir 30 seconds.

3. Add beef, carrots, broth, tomato paste, thyme, salt, pepper and bay leaves; bring to a boil over medium-high heat. Reduce heat to medium-low; cover and cook 2 hours or until beef is fork-tender. Add onions and green beans during last 30 minutes of cooking.

4. Remove and discard bay leaves. Stir water into flour in small bowl until smooth. Add mixture to stew; cook and stir 2 to 3 minutes or until thickened.

BROCCOLI CHEESE SOUP

MAKES 4 TO 6 SERVINGS

6 tablespoons (¾ stick) butter

1 cup chopped onion

1 clove garlic, minced

¼ cup all-purpose flour

2 cups vegetable broth

2 cups milk

1½ teaspoons Dijon mustard

½ teaspoon salt

¼ teaspoon ground nutmeg

¼ teaspoon black pepper

⅛ teaspoon hot pepper sauce

1 package (16 ounces) frozen broccoli (5 cups)

2 carrots, shredded (1 cup)

6 ounces pasteurized process cheese product, cubed

1 cup (4 ounces) shredded sharp Cheddar cheese, plus additional for garnish

1. Melt butter in large saucepan over medium-low heat. Add onion; cook and stir 10 minutes or until very soft. Add garlic; cook and stir 1 minute. Increase heat to medium. Whisk in flour until smooth; cook and stir 3 minutes without browning.

2. Gradually whisk in broth and milk. Add mustard, salt, nutmeg, black pepper and hot pepper sauce; cook 15 minutes or until thickened, stirring frequently.

3. Add broccoli; cook 15 minutes. Add carrots; cook 10 minutes or until vegetables are tender.

4. Transfer half of soup to food processor or blender; process until smooth. Return to saucepan. Add cheese product and 1 cup Cheddar; cook and stir over low heat until cheeses are melted. Ladle into bowls; garnish with additional Cheddar.

RUSTIC COUNTRY TURKEY SOUP

MAKES 4 SERVINGS

2 tablespoons olive oil

1 cup chopped onion

¾ cup sliced carrots

4 ounces sliced mushrooms

1 teaspoon minced garlic

2 cans (about 14 ounces each) chicken broth

2 ounces uncooked multigrain rotini pasta

1 teaspoon dried thyme or dried parsley flakes

½ teaspoon salt

¼ teaspoon poultry seasoning

⅛ teaspoon red pepper flakes

2 cups chopped cooked turkey breast

¼ cup chopped fresh parsley

1. Heat oil in large saucepan over medium-high heat. Add onion and carrots; cook and stir 3 minutes. Add mushrooms; cook 3 minutes, stirring occasionally. Add garlic; cook and stir 30 seconds. Stir in broth; bring to a boil.

2. Add pasta, thyme, salt, poultry seasoning and red pepper flakes; return to a boil. Reduce heat to medium; cover and cook 8 minutes or until pasta is tender.

3. Remove from heat; stir in turkey and fresh parsley. Cover and let stand 5 minutes before serving.

CREAMY TOMATO SOUP

MAKES 6 SERVINGS

3 tablespoons olive oil, divided

2 tablespoons butter

1 large onion, finely chopped

2 cloves garlic, minced

2 teaspoons sugar

1 teaspoon salt

½ teaspoon dried oregano

2 cans (28 ounces each) peeled Italian plum tomatoes, undrained

4 cups ½-inch focaccia cubes (half of 9-ounce loaf)

½ teaspoon black pepper

½ cup whipping cream

1. Heat 2 tablespoons oil and butter in large saucepan over medium-high heat. Add onion; cook and stir 5 minutes or until softened. Add garlic, sugar, salt and oregano; cook and stir 30 seconds. Stir in tomatoes with juice; bring to a boil. Reduce heat to medium-low; cook 45 minutes, stirring occasionally.

2. Meanwhile, prepare croutons. Preheat oven to 350°F. Combine focaccia cubes, remaining 1 tablespoon oil and pepper in large bowl; toss to coat. Spread on large baking sheet. Bake about 10 minutes or until bread cubes are golden brown.

3. Blend soup with immersion blender until smooth. (Or process in batches in food processor or blender.) Stir in cream; cook over low heat until heated through. Serve soup topped with croutons.

CHILE VERDE CHICKEN STEW

MAKES 6 SERVINGS

⅓ cup all-purpose flour

1½ teaspoons salt, divided

¼ teaspoon black pepper

1½ pounds boneless skinless chicken breasts, cut into 1½-inch pieces

4 tablespoons vegetable oil, divided

1 pound tomatillos (about 9), husked and halved

2 onions, chopped

2 cans (4 ounces each) diced mild green chiles

1 tablespoon dried oregano

1 tablespoon ground cumin

2 cloves garlic, minced

1 teaspoon sugar

2 cups chicken broth

8 ounces Mexican beer

5 unpeeled red potatoes, diced

Optional toppings: chopped fresh cilantro, sour cream, shredded Monterey Jack cheese, lime wedges, diced avocado and/or hot pepper sauce

1. Combine flour, 1 teaspoon salt and pepper in large bowl. Add chicken; toss to coat. Heat 2 tablespoons oil in large nonstick skillet over medium heat. Add chicken; cook until lightly browned on all sides, stirring occasionally. Transfer to large saucepan or Dutch oven.

2. Heat remaining 2 tablespoons oil in same skillet. Add tomatillos, onions, chiles, oregano, cumin, garlic, sugar and remaining ½ teaspoon salt; cook 20 minutes or until vegetables are softened, stirring occasionally. Stir in broth and beer. Working in batches, process mixture in food processor or blender until almost smooth.

3. Add tomatillo mixture and potatoes to saucepan with chicken; bring to a boil over medium-high heat. Reduce heat to low; cover and cook 1 hour or until potatoes are tender, stirring occasionally. Serve with desired toppings.

HEARTY MUSHROOM BARLEY SOUP

MAKES 8 TO 10 SERVINGS

9 cups chicken broth

1 package (16 ounces) sliced mushrooms

1 onion, chopped

2 carrots, chopped

2 stalks celery, chopped

½ cup uncooked pearl barley

½ ounce dried porcini mushrooms

3 cloves garlic, minced

1 teaspoon salt

½ teaspoon dried thyme

½ teaspoon black pepper

SLOW COOKER DIRECTIONS

Combine broth, sliced mushrooms, onion, carrots, celery, barley, porcini mushrooms, garlic, salt, thyme and pepper in slow cooker. Cover; cook on LOW 4 to 6 hours.

VARIATION: For extra flavor, add a beef or ham bone to the slow cooker with the rest of the ingredients.

BEEF VEGETABLE SOUP

MAKES 8 SERVINGS

1½ pounds cubed beef stew meat

¼ cup all-purpose flour

3 tablespoons vegetable oil, divided

1 onion, chopped

2 stalks celery, chopped

3 tablespoons tomato paste

2 teaspoons salt

1 teaspoon dried thyme

½ teaspoon garlic powder

¼ teaspoon black pepper

6 cups beef broth, divided

1 can (28 ounces) stewed tomatoes, undrained

1 tablespoon Worcestershire sauce

1 bay leaf

4 unpeeled red potatoes (about 1 pound), cut into 1-inch pieces

3 medium carrots, cut in half lengthwise then cut into ½-inch slices

6 ounces green beans, trimmed and cut into 1-inch pieces

1 cup frozen corn

1. Combine beef and flour in medium bowl; toss to coat. Heat 1 tablespoon oil in large saucepan or Dutch oven over medium-high heat. Cook beef in two batches about 5 minutes or until browned on all sides, adding additional 1 tablespoon oil after first batch. Remove to plate.

2. Heat remaining 1 tablespoon oil in same saucepan. Add onion and celery; cook and stir about 5 minutes or until softened. Add tomato paste, 2 teaspoons salt, thyme, garlic powder and ¼ teaspoon pepper; cook and stir 1 minute. Stir in 1 cup broth, scraping up browned bits from bottom of saucepan. Stir in remaining 5 cups broth, tomatoes, Worcestershire sauce, bay leaf and beef; bring to a boil.

3. Reduce heat to low; cover and cook 1 hour and 20 minutes. Add potatoes and carrots; cook 15 minutes. Add green beans and corn; cook 15 minutes or until vegetables are tender. Remove and discard bay leaf. Season with additional salt and pepper.

POULTRY

CHICKEN POT PIE

MAKES ABOUT 4 SERVINGS

1½ pounds bone-in chicken pieces, skinned

1 cup chicken broth

½ teaspoon salt

¼ teaspoon black pepper

1 to 1½ cups milk

3 tablespoons butter

1 medium onion, chopped

1 cup sliced celery

⅓ cup all-purpose flour

2 cups frozen mixed vegetables (broccoli, carrots and cauliflower), thawed

1 tablespoon chopped fresh Italian parsley *or* 1 teaspoon dried parsley flakes

½ teaspoon dried thyme

1 (9-inch) refrigerated pie crust (half of 15-ounce package)

1 egg, lightly beaten

1. Combine chicken, broth, salt and pepper in large saucepan over medium-high heat; bring to a boil. Reduce heat to low; cover and cook 30 minutes or until chicken is cooked through (165°F).

2. Remove chicken to plate; let stand until cool enough to handle. Pour broth into glass measure. Cool 15 minutes; spoon off fat. Add enough milk to equal 2½ cups. Remove chicken from bones; cut into ½-inch pieces.

3. Preheat oven to 400°F. Melt butter in same saucepan over medium heat. Add onion and celery; cook and stir 3 minutes or until vegetables are tender. Stir in flour until well blended. Gradually add broth mixture; cook until sauce boils and thickens, stirring constantly. Add chicken, vegetables, parsley and thyme; stir until blended. Pour into 1½-quart casserole.

4. Roll out pie crust to 1 inch larger than diameter of casserole on lightly floured surface. Cut slits in crust to vent; place on top of casserole. Roll edge and trim off extra dough; flute edge. If desired, reroll scraps and cut into decorative designs; place on crust. Brush with beaten egg.

5. Bake 30 minutes until crust is golden brown and filling is bubbly.

NOTE: You can substitute 2 cups diced cooked chicken for the chicken pieces. Increase chicken broth to 1 (14-ounce) can. Decrease salt to ¼ teaspoon. Combine broth, salt and pepper in glass measure. Add enough milk to equal 2½ cups. Proceed as directed in step 3.

CRISPY RANCH CHICKEN

MAKES 6 SERVINGS

1½ cups ranch salad dressing

1½ cups cornflake crumbs

1 teaspoon dried rosemary

½ teaspoon salt

½ teaspoon black pepper

3 pounds bone-in chicken pieces

1. Preheat oven to 375°F. Spray 13×9-inch baking dish with nonstick cooking spray.

2. Pour salad dressing into medium bowl. Combine cornflakes, rosemary, salt and pepper in shallow dish; mix well.

3. Dip chicken pieces in salad dressing, shaking off excess. Coat with cornflake mixture, pressing lightly to adhere. Place chicken in prepared baking dish.

4. Bake 50 to 55 minutes or until cooked through (165°F).

VARIATION: To add Italian flavor to this dish, substitute 1¼ cups Italian-seasoned dry bread crumbs and ¼ cup grated Parmesan cheese for the cornflake crumbs, rosemary, salt and pepper. Prepare as directed.

HERB ROASTED TURKEY

MAKES 8 TO 10 SERVINGS

½ cup coarse-grain or Dijon mustard

¼ cup chopped fresh sage

2 tablespoons chopped fresh thyme

2 tablespoons chopped fresh chives

1 small (8- to 10-pound) turkey, thawed if frozen

Salt and black pepper

1. Preheat oven to 450°F. Combine mustard, sage, thyme and chives in small bowl; mix well.

2. Pat turkey dry with paper towels. Carefully insert fingers under skin, beginning at neck cavity and sliding down over breast to form pocket between skin and turkey breast. Spoon mustard mixture into pocket; massage outside of skin to spread mixture into even layer.

3. Place turkey, breast side up, on rack in shallow roasting pan. Tie legs together with kitchen string. Season with salt and pepper.

4. Place turkey in oven. *Reduce oven temperature to 325°F.* Roast turkey 18 minutes per pound or until cooked through (165°F). Once turkey browns, tent with foil for remainder of roasting time. Remove turkey to cutting board; reserve pan drippings for gravy, if desired. Loosely tent turkey with foil; let stand 20 minutes before carving.

CREAMY BAKED CHICKEN WITH ARTICHOKES AND MUSHROOMS

MAKES 6 SERVINGS

6 boneless skinless chicken breasts (4 to 6 ounces each)

1½ teaspoons paprika

1½ teaspoons dried thyme

½ teaspoon salt

½ teaspoon black pepper

1 can (14 ounces) artichokes packed in water, drained and cut in half

1 tablespoon butter

1 package (8 ounces) sliced cremini mushrooms

2 tablespoons all-purpose flour

¾ cup chicken broth

½ cup half-and-half

1. Preheat oven to 375°F.

2. Place chicken in 13×9-inch baking dish. Combine paprika, thyme, salt and pepper in small bowl; mix well. Reserve 1 teaspoon seasoning mixture; sprinkle remaining seasoning mixture evenly over chicken. Arrange artichokes around chicken.

3. Melt butter in large saucepan over medium heat. Add mushrooms and reserved 1 teaspoon seasoning mixture; cook and stir 5 minutes or until mushrooms are tender. Sprinkle flour over mushrooms; cook and stir 1 minute. Stir in broth; cook and stir 3 minutes or until thickened. Stir in half-and-half; cook 1 minute. Pour over chicken and artichokes.

4. Bake 30 minutes or until chicken is no longer pink.

BBQ CHICKEN FLATBREAD

MAKES 4 SERVINGS

3 tablespoons red wine vinegar

2 teaspoons sugar

¼ red onion, thinly sliced (about ⅓ cup)

3 cups shredded rotisserie chicken

½ cup barbecue sauce

1 package (about 14 ounces) refrigerated pizza dough

All-purpose flour, for dusting

1½ cups (6 ounces) shredded mozzarella cheese

1 green onion, thinly sliced

2 tablespoons chopped fresh cilantro

1. Preheat oven to 400°F; place oven rack in lower third of oven. Line baking sheet with parchment paper.

2. For pickled onion, combine vinegar and sugar in small bowl; stir until sugar is dissolved. Add red onion; cover and let stand at room temperature while preparing flatbread. Combine chicken and barbecue sauce in medium bowl; toss to coat.

3. Unroll dough on lightly floured surface; roll into 11×9-inch rectangle. Transfer to prepared baking sheet; top with cheese and chicken mixture.

4. Bake about 12 minutes or until crust is golden brown and crisp and cheese is melted. Drain liquid from red onion; sprinkle over flatbread. Top with green onion and cilantro. Serve immediately.

CHICKEN SCARPIELLO

MAKES 4 TO 6 SERVINGS

3 tablespoons extra virgin olive oil, divided

1 pound spicy Italian sausage, cut into 1-inch pieces

1 cut-up whole chicken (about 3 pounds)*

1 teaspoon salt, divided

1 large onion, chopped

2 red, yellow or orange bell peppers, cut into ¼-inch strips

3 cloves garlic, minced

½ cup dry white wine such as sauvignon blanc

½ cup chicken broth

½ cup coarsely chopped seeded hot cherry peppers

½ cup liquid from cherry pepper jar

1 teaspoon dried oregano

¼ cup chopped fresh Italian parsley

*Or purchase 2 bone-in chicken leg quarters and 2 chicken breasts; separate drumsticks and thighs and cut breasts in half.

1. Heat 1 tablespoon oil in large skillet over medium-high heat. Add sausage; cook about 10 minutes or until well browned on all sides, stirring occasionally. Remove to plate.

2. Heat 1 tablespoon oil in same skillet. Sprinkle chicken with ½ teaspoon salt; arrange skin side down in single layer in skillet (cook in batches if necessary). Cook about 6 minutes per side or until browned. Remove to plate. Drain fat from skillet.

3. Heat remaining 1 tablespoon oil in skillet. Add onion and remaining ½ teaspoon salt; cook and stir 2 minutes or until onion is softened, scraping up browned bits from bottom of skillet. Add bell peppers and garlic; cook and stir 5 minutes. Stir in wine; cook until liquid is reduced by half. Stir in broth, cherry peppers, cherry pepper liquid, oregano and salt and black pepper to taste; bring to a simmer.

4. Return sausage and chicken along with any accumulated juices to skillet. Partially cover skillet and cook 10 minutes. Uncover; cook 15 minutes or until chicken is cooked through (165°F). Sprinkle with parsley.

TIP: If too much liquid remains in the skillet when the chicken is cooked through, remove the chicken and sausage and continue simmering the sauce to reduce it slightly.

PULLED TURKEY SANDWICHES

MAKES 4 SERVINGS

- 1 tablespoon vegetable oil
- 1 small red onion, chopped
- 1 stalk celery, trimmed and chopped
- 3 cups coarsely chopped cooked turkey meat
- 1 can (8 ounces) tomato sauce
- ¼ cup ketchup
- 2 tablespoons packed brown sugar
- 1 tablespoon cider vinegar
- 2 teaspoons Worcestershire sauce
- 1 teaspoon Dijon mustard
- ¼ teaspoon chipotle chili powder
- ⅛ teaspoon salt
- 4 hamburger buns

1. Heat oil in large skillet or saucepan over medium-high heat. Add onion and celery; cook and stir 5 minutes or until vegetables are tender.

2. Stir in turkey, tomato sauce, ketchup, brown sugar, cider vinegar, Worcestershire sauce, mustard, chili powder and salt; cover and cook 45 minutes.

3. Serve turkey mixture on buns.

TIP: The pulled turkey filling for these sandwiches freezes well. Try doubling the recipe and freezing any leftovers. Before serving, thaw the filling in the refrigerator and reheat in the microwave.

OLD-FASHIONED CHICKEN AND DUMPLINGS

MAKES 6 SERVINGS

3 tablespoons butter

3 to 3½ pounds chicken pieces

3 cans (about 14 ounces each) chicken broth

3½ cups water

1 teaspoon salt

¼ teaspoon white pepper

2 large carrots, cut into 1-inch slices

2 stalks celery, cut into 1-inch slices

8 to 10 pearl onions, peeled

4 ounces small mushrooms, cut into halves

Parsley Dumplings (recipe follows)

½ cup frozen peas, thawed and drained

1. Melt butter in Dutch oven over medium-high heat. Add chicken; cook until browned on all sides.

2. Add broth, water, salt and pepper; bring to a boil over high heat. Reduce heat to low; cover and cook 15 minutes. Add carrots, celery, onions and mushrooms; cover and cook 40 minutes or until chicken and vegetables are tender.

3. Prepare Parsley Dumplings. When chicken is tender, skim fat from broth. Stir in peas. Drop dumpling mixture into broth, making 12 dumplings. Cover and cook 15 to 20 minutes or until dumplings are firm to the touch and toothpick inserted into centers comes out clean.

PARSLEY DUMPLINGS: Sift 2 cups all-purpose flour, 4 teaspoons baking powder and 1 teaspoon salt into medium bowl. Cut in 5 tablespoons cold butter with pastry blender or two knives until mixture resembles coarse crumbs. Make well in center; pour in 1 cup milk. Add 2 tablespoons chopped fresh parsley; stir with fork until mixture forms a ball.

PIZZA CHICKEN BAKE

MAKES 4 SERVINGS

3½ cups uncooked bowtie pasta

1 tablespoon vegetable oil

1 cup sliced mushrooms

1 jar (26 ounces) herb-flavored pasta sauce

1 teaspoon pizza seasoning blend

3 boneless skinless chicken breasts (about 12 ounces), quartered

1 cup (4 ounces) shredded mozzarella cheese

1. Preheat oven to 350°F. Spray 2-quart round baking dish with nonstick cooking spray. Cook pasta according to package directions until al dente. Drain and place in prepared dish.

2. Heat oil in large skillet over medium-high heat. Add mushrooms; cook and stir 5 minutes. Remove from heat; stir in pasta sauce and pizza seasoning.

3. Pour half of pasta sauce mixture into casserole; stir until pasta is well coated. Top with chicken and remaining pasta sauce mixture.

4. Cover and bake 50 minutes or until chicken is no longer pink in center. Remove from oven; sprinkle with cheese. Cover and let stand 5 minutes before serving.

TIP: Serve this casserole with grated Parmesan cheese and red pepper flakes so everyone can add their own individual pizza seasonings.

TURKEY AND VEGGIE MEATBALLS

MAKES 6 SERVINGS

1 pound ground turkey

½ cup finely chopped green onions

½ cup finely chopped green bell pepper

⅓ cup old-fashioned oats

¼ cup shredded carrot

¼ cup grated Parmesan cheese

1 egg

2 cloves garlic, minced

½ teaspoon salt

½ teaspoon Italian seasoning

¼ teaspoon fennel seeds

⅛ teaspoon red pepper flakes

1 tablespoon extra virgin olive oil

Marinara sauce, heated

1. Combine turkey, green onions, bell pepper, oats, carrot, cheese, egg, garlic, salt, Italian seasoning, fennel seeds and red pepper flakes in large bowl; mix well. Shape into 36 (1-inch) balls.

2. Heat oil in large nonstick skillet over medium-high heat. Add meatballs; cook about 11 minutes or until no longer pink in center, turning frequently. Serve immediately with marinara sauce or cool meatballs and freeze.*

*To freeze, cool completely and place in gallon-size resealable food storage bag. Release any excess air from bag and seal. Freeze bag flat for easier storage and faster thawing. This will also allow you to remove as many meatballs as needed without them sticking together. To reheat, place meatballs in a 12×8-inch microwavable dish and cook on HIGH 20 to 30 seconds or until hot.

FORTY-CLOVE CHICKEN FILICE

MAKES 4 TO 6 SERVINGS

¼ cup olive oil

1 cut-up whole chicken (about 3 pounds)

40 cloves garlic (about 2 heads), peeled

4 stalks celery, thickly sliced

½ cup dry white wine

¼ cup dry vermouth

Grated peel and juice of 1 lemon

2 tablespoons finely chopped fresh parsley

2 teaspoons dried basil

1 teaspoon dried oregano

Pinch of red pepper flakes

Salt and black pepper

1. Preheat oven to 375°F.

2. Heat oil in Dutch oven over medium heat. Add chicken; cook until browned on all sides.

3. Add garlic, celery, wine, vermouth, lemon juice, lemon peel, parsley, basil, oregano and red pepper flakes. Season with salt and black pepper.

4. Cover and bake 40 minutes. Uncover; bake 15 minutes or until chicken is cooked through (165°F).

OVEN BARBECUE CHICKEN

MAKES 4 TO 6 SERVINGS

1 cup barbecue sauce

¼ cup honey

2 tablespoons soy sauce

2 teaspoons grated
   fresh ginger

½ teaspoon dry mustard

1 cut-up whole chicken
   (about 3½ pounds)

1. Preheat oven to 350°F. Spray 13×9-inch baking dish or baking sheet with nonstick cooking spray.

2. Combine barbecue sauce, honey, soy sauce, ginger and mustard in small bowl; mix well. Place chicken in prepared baking dish; brush with sauce mixture.

3. Bake 45 minutes or until cooked through (165°F), brushing occasionally with sauce.

SOUTHWEST TURKEY BAKE

MAKES 8 SERVINGS

1 pound ground turkey

1 can (about 15 ounces) black beans, rinsed and drained

1 cup salsa

½ teaspoon ground cumin

⅛ teaspoon ground red pepper

1 package (8½ ounces) corn muffin mix

¾ cup chicken broth

1 egg

¾ cup (3 ounces) shredded Mexican cheese blend

Lime wedges (optional)

1. Preheat oven to 400°F. Brown turkey in large nonstick skillet over medium-high heat until no longer pink, stirring to break up meat. Stir in beans, salsa, cumin and red pepper; cook 2 minutes. Transfer to 13×9-inch baking dish.

2. Combine corn muffin mix, broth and egg in medium bowl; mix well. Spread over turkey mixture. Sprinkle with cheese.

3. Bake 15 minutes or until edges are lightly browned. Serve with lime wedges, if desired.

CHICKEN SCALOPPINE WITH MUSHROOMS AND ARTICHOKES

MAKES 4 SERVINGS

½ cup all-purpose flour

½ teaspoon salt

¼ teaspoon black pepper

4 boneless skinless chicken breasts (about 6 ounces each)

5 tablespoons butter, divided

2 tablespoons olive oil, divided

1 package (3 to 4 ounces) diced pancetta *or* ⅓ cup diced prosciutto

1 pound sliced mushrooms

1 can (14 ounces) artichoke hearts, sliced

3 tablespoons capers, rinsed and drained

⅓ cup lemon juice

3 tablespoons dry white wine

¾ cup whipping cream

2 teaspoons cornstarch

¾ cup chicken broth

1 package (16 ounces) angel hair pasta, cooked and drained

Chopped fresh parsley (optional)

1. Preheat oven to 250°F. Line baking sheet with foil. Combine flour, ½ teaspoon salt and ¼ teaspoon pepper in shallow dish. Pound chicken to ⅛-inch thickness between sheets of waxed paper with meat mallet or rolling pin. Cut each chicken breast in half crosswise. Coat both sides of chicken with flour mixture, shaking off excess.

2. Heat 1 tablespoon butter and 1 tablespoon oil in large skillet over medium-high heat. Add chicken in single layer; cook about 3 minutes per side or until golden brown. (Cook chicken in batches if necessary.) Remove to prepared baking sheet; place in oven to keep warm.

3. Add pancetta to skillet; cook and stir over medium heat 3 minutes or until lightly browned, scraping up browned bits from bottom of skillet. Add mushrooms; cook about 8 minutes or until mushrooms begin to brown, stirring occasionally. (Add additional 1 tablespoon oil if necessary to cook mushrooms.) Stir in artichokes and capers; cook 4 minutes. Reduce heat to low while preparing sauce.

4. Combine lemon juice and wine in small saucepan; bring to a boil over medium-high heat. Boil until reduced by one third. Stir in cream; cook over medium heat 4 minutes or until slightly thickened. Stir cornstarch into broth in small bowl until blended. Add to saucepan; cook and stir 3 minutes or until sauce thickens. Add remaining 4 tablespoons butter, 1 tablespoon at a time, whisking until sauce is smooth and well blended. Add sauce to mushroom mixture; cook and stir until heated through. Season with additional pepper.

5. Divide pasta among four plates; top with mushroom mixture and chicken. Garnish with parsley.

LEMON ROSEMARY ROASTED CHICKEN AND POTATOES

MAKES 4 SERVINGS

- 4 bone-in skin-on chicken breasts
- ½ cup lemon juice
- 6 tablespoons olive oil, divided
- 6 cloves garlic, minced, divided
- 2 tablespoons plus 1 teaspoon chopped fresh rosemary leaves *or* 2¼ teaspoons dried rosemary, divided
- 1½ teaspoons salt, divided
- 2 pounds unpeeled small red potatoes, cut into quarters
- 1 large onion, cut into 2-inch chunks
- ¼ teaspoon black pepper

1. Place chicken in large resealable food storage bag. Combine lemon juice, 3 tablespoons oil, 3 cloves garlic, 1 tablespoon rosemary and ½ teaspoon salt in small bowl; pour over chicken. Seal bag; turn to coat. Refrigerate several hours or overnight.

2. Preheat oven to 400°F. Combine potatoes and onion in roasting pan or on baking sheet. Combine remaining 3 tablespoons oil, 3 cloves garlic, 1 tablespoon rosemary, 1 teaspoon salt and pepper in small bowl; mix well. Pour over vegetables; toss to coat.

3. Drain chicken; discard marinade. Arrange chicken in pan with vegetables in single layer; sprinkle with remaining 1 teaspoon rosemary.

4. Roast about 50 minutes or until potatoes are tender and chicken is cooked through (165°F). Sprinkle with additional salt and pepper to taste.

CHUCK
RIB
SHORT LOIN
SIRLOIN
RUMP
BRISKET
PLATE
FLANK
ROUND
SHANK
SHANK

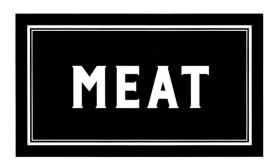

MEAT

SAGE-ROASTED PORK WITH RUTABAGA

MAKES 4 TO 6 SERVINGS

1 bunch fresh sage

4 cloves garlic, minced
(2 tablespoons)

1½ teaspoons coarse salt,
divided

1 teaspoon coarsely ground
black pepper, divided

5 tablespoons extra virgin
olive oil, divided

1 boneless pork loin roast
(2 to 2½ pounds)

2 medium or 1 large rutabaga
(1 to 1½ pounds)

4 carrots, cut into 1½-inch
pieces

1. Chop enough sage to measure 2 tablespoons; reserve remaining sage. Mash chopped sage, garlic, ½ teaspoon salt and ½ teaspoon pepper in small bowl to form paste. Stir in 2 tablepoons oil.

2. Score fatty side of pork roast with sharp knife, making cuts about ¼ inch deep. Rub herb paste into cuts and over all sides of pork. Place pork on large plate; cover and refrigerate 1 to 2 hours.

3. Preheat oven to 400°F. Spray large roasting pan with nonstick cooking spray. Cut rutabaga into halves or quarters; peel and cut into 1½-inch pieces. Combine rutabaga and carrots in large bowl. Drizzle with remaining 3 tablespoons oil and sprinkle with remaining 1 teaspoon salt and ½ teaspoon pepper; toss to coat.

4. Arrange vegetables in single layer in prepared pan. Place pork on top of vegetables, scraping any remaining herb paste from plate into roasting pan. Tuck 3 sprigs of remaining sage into vegetables.

5. Roast 15 minutes. *Reduce oven temperature to 325°F.* Roast 45 minutes to 1 hour 15 minutes or until pork is 145°F and barely pink in center, stirring vegetables once or twice during cooking time. Remove pork to cutting board; tent with foil. Let stand 5 minutes before slicing.

CLASSIC LASAGNA
MAKES 6 TO 8 SERVINGS

1 tablespoon olive oil

8 ounces bulk mild Italian sausage

8 ounces ground beef

1 medium onion, chopped

3 cloves garlic, minced, divided

1½ teaspoons salt, divided

1 can (28 ounces) crushed tomatoes

1 can (28 ounces) diced tomatoes

2 teaspoons Italian seasoning

1 egg

1 container (15 ounces) ricotta cheese

¾ cup grated Parmesan cheese, divided

½ cup minced fresh parsley

¼ teaspoon black pepper

12 uncooked no-boil lasagna noodles

4 cups (16 ounces) shredded mozzarella

1. Preheat oven to 350°F. Spray 13×9-inch baking dish with nonstick cooking spray.

2. Heat oil in large saucepan over medium-high heat. Add sausage, beef, onion, 2 cloves garlic and 1 teaspoon salt; cook and stir 10 minutes or until meat is no longer pink, breaking up meat with wooden spoon. Add crushed tomatoes, diced tomatoes and Italian seasoning; bring to a boil. Reduce heat to medium low; cook 15 minutes, stirring occasionally.

3. Meanwhile, beat egg in medium bowl. Stir in ricotta, ½ cup Parmesan, parsley, remaining 1 clove garlic, ½ teaspoon salt and pepper until well blended.

4. Spread ¼ cup sauce in prepared baking dish. Top with 3 noodles, breaking to fit if necessary. Spread one third of ricotta mixture over noodles. Sprinkle with 1 cup mozzarella; top with 2 cups sauce. Repeat layers of noodles, ricotta mixture, mozzarella and sauce two times. Top with remaining 3 noodles, sauce, 1 cup mozzarella and ¼ cup Parmesan. Cover dish with foil sprayed with cooking spray.

5. Bake 30 minutes. Remove foil; bake 10 to 15 minutes or until hot and bubbly. Let stand 10 minutes before serving.

BBQ BABY BACK RIBS

MAKES 4 SERVINGS

1¼ cups water

1 cup white vinegar

⅔ cup packed dark brown sugar

½ cup tomato paste

1 tablespoon yellow mustard

1½ teaspoons salt

1 teaspoon liquid smoke

1 teaspoon onion powder

½ teaspoon garlic powder

½ teaspoon paprika

2 racks pork baby back ribs (3½ to 4 pounds total)

1. Combine water, vinegar, brown sugar, tomato paste, mustard, salt, liquid smoke, onion powder, garlic powder and paprika in medium saucepan; bring to a boil over medium heat. Reduce heat to medium-low; cook 40 minutes or until sauce thickens, stirring occasionally.

2. Preheat oven to 300°F. Place each rack of ribs on large sheet of heavy-duty foil. Brush some of sauce over ribs, covering completely. Fold down edges of foil tightly to seal and create packet; arrange packets on baking sheet, seam sides up.

3. Bake 2 hours. Prepare grill or preheat broiler. Carefully drain off excess liquid from rib packets.

4. Brush ribs with sauce; grill or broil about 5 minutes per side or until beginning to char, brushing with sauce once or twice during grilling. Serve with remaining sauce.

SAVORY STEAK AND MUSHROOMS

MAKES 4 SERVINGS

¾ cup water

3 tablespoons Worcestershire sauce

3 tablespoons soy sauce

1½ tablespoons chili powder

5 cloves garlic, minced, divided

2 teaspoons onion powder

2 teaspoons paprika

1½ teaspoons ground red pepper

1¼ teaspoons black pepper, divided

4 top sirloin steaks (about 8 ounces each, 1 inch thick)

4 tablespoons (½ stick) butter, divided

2 tablespoons olive oil

2 onions, thinly sliced

16 ounces sliced mushrooms (white and shiitake or all white)

¾ teaspoon salt, divided

1. Combine water, Worcestershire sauce, soy sauce, chili powder, 3 cloves garlic, onion powder, paprika, red pepper and 1 teaspoon black pepper in small bowl; mix well. Place steaks in large resealable food storage bag; pour marinade over steaks. Seal bag; turn to coat. Marinate in refrigerator 1 to 3 hours, turning occasionally.

2. Remove steaks from marinade 30 minutes before cooking; discard marinade and pat steaks dry with paper towel. Prepare grill for direct cooking. Oil grid.

3. While grill is preheating, heat 1 tablespoon butter and oil in large skillet over medium-high heat. Add onions; cook 5 minutes, stirring occasionally. Add mushrooms; cook 10 minutes or until onions are golden brown and mushrooms are beginning to brown, stirring occasionally. Stir in ½ teaspoon salt and remaining ¼ teaspoon black pepper. Combine remaining 3 tablespoons butter, 2 cloves garlic and ¼ teaspoon salt in small skillet; cook over medium-low heat 3 minutes or until garlic begins to sizzle.

4. Grill steaks over medium-high heat 6 minutes; turn and grill 6 minutes for medium rare or until desired doneness. Brush both sides of steaks with garlic butter during last 2 minutes of cooking. Remove to plate; tent with foil. Let stand 5 minutes. Serve steaks with onion and mushroom mixture.

PULLED PORK SANDWICHES

MAKES 6 TO 8 SERVINGS

2 tablespoons coarse salt

2 tablespoons packed
   brown sugar

2 tablespoons paprika

1 teaspoon dry mustard

1 teaspoon black pepper

1 boneless pork shoulder
   roast (about 3 pounds)

1½ cups dark beer

½ cup cider vinegar

6 to 8 large hamburger buns,
   split

¾ cup barbecue sauce

1. Preheat oven to 325°F. Combine salt, brown sugar, paprika, mustard and pepper in small bowl; mix well. Rub mixture all over pork.

2. Place pork in Dutch oven; add beer and vinegar.

3. Cover and bake 3 hours or until pork is fork-tender. Let stand 15 to 30 minutes or until cool enough to handle.

4. Shred pork into bite-size pieces. Serve on buns with barbecue sauce.

CHILI SPAGHETTI CASSEROLE

MAKES 8 SERVINGS

8 ounces uncooked spaghetti

1 pound ground beef

1 medium onion, chopped

½ teaspoon salt

⅛ teaspoon black pepper

1 can (about 15 ounces) vegetarian chili with beans

1 can (about 14 ounces) Italian-style stewed tomatoes

1½ cups (6 ounces) shredded sharp Cheddar cheese, divided

½ cup sour cream

1½ teaspoons chili powder

¼ teaspoon garlic powder

1. Preheat oven to 350°F. Spray 13×9-inch baking dish with nonstick cooking spray.

2. Cook spaghetti according to package directions; drain and place in prepared baking dish.

3. Meanwhile, combine beef, onion, salt and pepper in large skillet. Brown beef over medium-high heat 6 to 8 minutes, stirring to break up meat. Drain fat. Stir in chili, tomatoes, 1 cup cheese, sour cream, chili powder and garlic powder; mix well.

4. Add chili mixture to spaghetti; stir gently to coat. Sprinkle with remaining ½ cup cheese.

5. Cover with foil and bake 30 minutes or until hot and bubbly. Let stand 5 minutes before serving.

YANKEE POT ROAST

MAKES 10 TO 12 SERVINGS

1 boneless beef chuck pot roast (2½ pounds), trimmed

Salt and black pepper

3 unpeeled baking potatoes (about 1 pound), cut into quarters

2 carrots, cut into ¾-inch slices

2 stalks celery, cut into ¾-inch slices

1 onion, sliced

1 parsnip, cut into ¾-inch slices

2 bay leaves

1 teaspoon dried rosemary

½ teaspoon dried thyme

½ cup beef broth

SLOW COOKER DIRECTIONS

1. Cut beef into ¾-inch pieces; sprinkle with salt and pepper.

2. Combine potatoes, carrots, celery, onion, parsnip, bay leaves, rosemary and thyme in slow cooker. Top with beef. Pour broth over beef.

3. Cover; cook on LOW 8½ to 9 hours or until beef is fork-tender. Remove beef and vegetables to serving platter. Remove and discard bay leaves.

TIP: To make gravy, pour the cooking liquid into a 2-cup measure; let stand 5 minutes. Skim off fat. Bring the cooking liquid to a boil in a small saucepan over medium-high heat. For each cup of cooking liquid, stir 2 tablespoons flour into ¼ cup cold water in a small bowl until smooth; add to the boiling cooking liquid. Cook and stir 1 minute or until thickened.

BAKED HAM WITH SWEET AND SPICY GLAZE

MAKES 8 TO 10 SERVINGS

1 (8-pound) bone-in smoked
half ham

Sweet and Spicy Glaze
(recipe follows)

1. Preheat oven to 325°F. Place ham, fat side up, in roasting pan. Bake 3 hours.

2. Meanwhile, prepare Sweet and Spicy Glaze. Remove ham from oven; generously brush half of glaze over ham. Bake 30 minutes or until ham is 160°F.

3. Remove ham from oven; brush with remaining glaze. Let stand about 20 minutes before slicing.

SWEET AND SPICY GLAZE

MAKES ABOUT 2 CUPS

¾ cup packed brown sugar
⅓ cup cider vinegar
¼ cup golden raisins
1 can (8¾ ounces) sliced
peaches in heavy syrup,
drained, chopped and
syrup reserved
1 tablespoon cornstarch
¼ cup orange juice

1 can (8¼ ounces) crushed
pineapple in syrup,
undrained
1 tablespoon grated
orange peel
1 clove garlic, minced
½ teaspoon red pepper flakes
½ teaspoon grated
fresh ginger

1. Combine brown sugar, vinegar, raisins and peach syrup in medium saucepan; bring to a boil over high heat. Reduce heat to low; cook 8 to 10 minutes.

2. Whisk cornstarch into orange juice in small bowl until smooth. Stir into brown sugar mixture. Stir in peaches, pineapple, orange peel, garlic, red pepper flakes and ginger; bring to a boil over medium heat. Cook until thickened, stirring constantly.

SOUTHWESTERN SLOPPY JOES

MAKES 8 SERVINGS

1 pound ground beef

1 cup chopped onion

¼ cup chopped celery

¼ cup water

1 can (10 ounces) diced tomatoes with green chiles

1 can (8 ounces) tomato sauce

4 teaspoons packed brown sugar

½ teaspoon salt

½ teaspoon ground cumin

8 whole wheat hamburger buns, split

1. Combine beef, onion, celery and water in large skillet; cook over medium-high heat 6 to 8 minutes or until beef is no longer pink. Drain fat.

2. Stir in tomatoes, tomato sauce, brown sugar, salt and cumin; bring to a boil over high heat. Reduce heat to low; cook 20 minutes or until mixture thickens, stirring occasionally. Serve on buns.

FAMILY-STYLE FRANKFURTERS WITH RICE AND BEANS

MAKES 6 SERVINGS

- 1 tablespoon vegetable oil
- 1 onion, chopped
- ½ green bell pepper, chopped
- 2 cloves garlic, minced
- 1 can (about 15 ounces) red kidney beans, rinsed and drained
- 1 can (about 15 ounces) Great Northern beans, rinsed and drained
- 8 ounces beef frankfurters, cut into ¼-inch slices
- 1 cup uncooked instant brown rice
- 1 cup vegetable broth
- ¼ cup packed brown sugar
- ¼ cup ketchup
- 3 tablespoons dark molasses
- 1 tablespoon Dijon mustard

1. Preheat oven to 350°F. Spray 13×9-inch baking dish with nonstick cooking spray.

2. Heat oil in large saucepan over medium-high heat. Add onion, bell pepper and garlic; cook and stir 3 minutes or until vegetables are tender.

3. Add beans, frankfurters, rice, broth, brown sugar, ketchup, molasses and mustard to saucepan; stir gently until blended. Transfer to prepared baking dish.

4. Cover and bake 30 minutes or until rice is tender.

CHIPOTLE STRIP STEAKS

MAKES 4 SERVINGS

1 tablespoon olive oil

⅓ cup finely chopped onion

¾ cup beer

1 teaspoon Worcestershire sauce

⅓ cup ketchup

1 tablespoon red wine vinegar

1 teaspoon sugar

⅛ to ¼ teaspoon chipotle chili powder

4 bone-in strip steaks (about 8 ounces each)

1 teaspoon salt

1. Heat oil in small saucepan over medium-high heat. Add onion; cook 3 minutes or until softened, stirring occasionally. Add beer and Worcestershire sauce; bring to a boil, stirring occasionally. Cook until reduced to about ⅓ cup. Stir in ketchup, vinegar, sugar and chili powder; cook over medium-low heat 3 minutes or until thickened, stirring occasionally. Keep warm.

2. Prepare grill for direct cooking over medium-high heat. Oil grid. Sprinkle steaks with salt.

3. Grill steaks 4 to 5 minutes per side for medium rare or until desired doneness. Serve with chipotle sauce.

PORK SCHNITZEL WITH MUSHROOM GRAVY

MAKES 6 SERVINGS

6 thin-cut boneless pork sirloin chops or boneless pork loin chops (about 1¼ pounds)*

Salt and black pepper

½ cup plus 1 tablespoon all-purpose flour, divided

2 eggs, beaten

1 cup plain dry bread crumbs

2 tablespoons chopped fresh parsley *or* 1 tablespoon dried parsley flakes

¼ cup vegetable oil

4 tablespoons (½ stick) butter, divided

¼ cup finely chopped onion

1 package (8 ounces) sliced button mushrooms

1 cup chicken broth

2 to 3 tablespoons half-and-half

Pork cutlets can be substituted for the boneless pork chops.

1. Pound pork chops with meat mallet to ¼-inch thickness. Season with salt and pepper. Place ½ cup flour in shallow dish. Lightly beat eggs in separate shallow dish. Combine bread crumbs and parsley in third shallow dish.

2. Coat pork chops with flour, shaking off excess. Dip in eggs, then in bread crumb mixture, turning to coat.

3. Heat oil and 2 tablespoons butter in large skillet over medium heat. Add pork in two batches; cook 3 minutes per side or until browned. Remove to plate; tent with foil.

4. Melt remaining 2 tablespoons butter in same skillet over medium heat. Add onion; cook and stir 1 minute. Add mushrooms; cook and stir 6 to 7 minutes or until mushrooms are lightly browned and most of liquid has evaporated. Stir in remaining 1 tablespoon flour; cook 1 minute. Add broth; bring to a boil, stirring constantly. Boil 1 minute. Remove from heat; stir in half-and-half.

5. Spoon gravy over pork. Serve immediately.

CLASSIC CHILI

MAKES 6 SERVINGS

1½ pounds ground beef

1½ cups chopped onion

1 cup chopped green
   bell pepper

2 cloves garlic, minced

3 cans (about 15 ounces
   each) dark red kidney
   beans, rinsed and drained

2 cans (about 15 ounces
   each) tomato sauce

1 can (about 14 ounces)
   diced tomatoes

2 to 3 teaspoons chili powder

1 to 2 teaspoons dry
   hot mustard

¾ teaspoon dried basil

½ teaspoon black pepper

1 to 2 dried hot chile peppers
   (optional)

Shredded Cheddar cheese
   (optional)

Fresh cilantro leaves
   (optional)

SLOW COOKER DIRECTIONS

1. Cook and stir beef, onion, bell pepper and garlic in large skillet over medium-high heat 6 to 8 minutes or until beef is browned and onion is tender. Drain fat. Transfer to slow cooker.

2. Add beans, tomato sauce, tomatoes, chili powder, mustard, basil, black pepper and chile peppers, if desired, to slow cooker; mix well.

3. Cover; cook on LOW 8 to 10 hours or on HIGH 4 to 5 hours. Remove and discard chiles before serving. Serve with cheese, if desired. Garnish with cilantro.

HAM AND BARBECUED BEAN SKILLET

MAKES 4 SERVINGS

1 tablespoon vegetable oil

1 cup chopped onion

1 teaspoon minced garlic

1 can (about 15 ounces) kidney beans, rinsed and drained

1 can (about 15 ounces) cannellini or Great Northern beans, rinsed and drained

1 cup chopped green bell pepper

½ cup packed brown sugar

½ cup ketchup

2 tablespoons cider vinegar

2 teaspoons dry mustard

1 ham steak (½ inch thick, about 12 ounces), cut into ½-inch pieces

1. Heat oil in large skillet over medium-high heat. Add onion and garlic; cook and stir 3 minutes. Add beans, bell pepper, brown sugar, ketchup, vinegar and mustard; mix well.

2. Add ham to skillet. Reduce heat to low; cook about 8 minutes or until sauce thickens and mixture is heated through, stirring occasionally.

VEGETABLES & SIDES

ORANGE AND MAPLE GLAZED ROASTED BEETS

MAKES 4 SERVINGS

4 medium beets, scrubbed

2 teaspoons olive oil

¼ cup orange juice

3 tablespoons balsamic or cider vinegar

2 tablespoons maple syrup

2 teaspoons grated orange peel, divided

1 teaspoon Dijon mustard

1 to 2 tablespoons chopped fresh mint (optional)

Salt and black pepper

1. Preheat oven to 425°F. Place beets in medium baking dish. Drizzle with oil; toss to coat.

2. Cover and roast 45 minutes to 1 hour or until knife inserted into largest beet goes in easily. Let stand until cool enough to handle.

3. Peel beets. Cut in half lengthwise, then cut into wedges. Return to baking dish.

4. Whisk orange juice, vinegar, maple syrup, 1 teaspoon orange peel and mustard in small bowl until well blended. Pour over beets.

5. Roast, uncovered, 10 to 15 minutes or until heated through and all liquid is absorbed. Sprinkle with remaining 1 teaspoon orange peel and mint, if desired. Season with salt and pepper.

CREAMY LAYERED VEGETABLE BAKE

MAKES 8 SERVINGS

2 large eggplants

4 teaspoons salt, divided

5 tablespoons olive oil, divided

½ teaspoon black pepper

½ cup chopped onion

2 medium zucchini, thinly sliced

1 package (8 ounces) sliced mushrooms

1 tablespoon Italian seasoning

2 teaspoons minced garlic, divided

1 container (15 ounces) ricotta cheese

¾ cup shredded Parmesan cheese, divided

1 egg, lightly beaten

12 ounces fresh mozzarella cheese, thinly sliced

⅓ cup butter

3 tablespoons cornstarch

1¾ cups milk

1. Peel eggplants; cut off and discard ends. Cut each eggplant vertically into six equal slices. Place slices in large colander set over bowl; sprinkle with 2 teaspoons salt. Let stand 30 minutes. Rinse eggplant slices under cold water; pat dry with paper towels.

2. Preheat oven to 400°F. Arrange eggplant slices in single layer on baking sheets. Brush both sides of slices with 4 tablespoons oil; sprinkle with 1 teaspoon salt and pepper. Bake 20 minutes or until golden brown and tender, turning halfway through cooking time. *Reduce oven temperature to 350°F.* Spray 13×9-inch baking dish with nonstick cooking spray.

3. Meanwhile, heat remaining 1 tablespoon oil in large skillet over medium heat. Add onion; cook and stir 3 minutes. Add zucchini, mushrooms, Italian seasoning, 1 teaspoon garlic and ½ teaspoon salt; cook and stir 5 to 7 minutes or until vegetables are tender.

4. Combine ricotta, ¼ cup Parmesan and egg in medium bowl; mix well.

5. Arrange eggplant slices in single layer in bottom of prepared dish. Layer with half of mozzarella, half of zucchini mixture and half of ricotta mixture. Repeat layers.

6. Melt butter in medium saucepan over medium heat. Add remaining 1 teaspoon garlic; cook and stir 1 minute. Whisk in cornstarch; cook 1 minute. Gradually add milk; whisk 2 to 3 minutes or until sauce is thickened. Season with remaining ½ teaspoon salt. Pour sauce over vegetables and cheese; top with remaining ½ cup Parmesan.

7. Bake 30 minutes or until heated through and cheese is melted. Let stand 10 to 15 minutes before serving.

KALE WITH MUSHROOMS AND BACON

MAKES 4 SERVINGS

2 slices bacon, chopped

½ cup sliced shallots

1 package (4 ounces) sliced mixed exotic mushrooms *or* 8 ounces cremini mushrooms, sliced

10 cups loosely packed torn fresh kale leaves (about 8 ounces), tough stems removed

2 tablespoons water

½ teaspoon black pepper

1. Cook bacon in large skillet over medium heat 5 minutes. Add shallots; cook and stir 3 minutes. Add mushrooms; cook and stir 8 minutes.

2. Add kale and water; cover and cook 5 minutes. Uncover; cook and stir 5 minutes or until kale is crisp-tender. Season with pepper.

ASPARAGUS AND ARUGULA SALAD

MAKES 4 TO 6 SERVINGS

½ cup sun-dried tomatoes (not packed in oil)

1 cup boiling water

1 cup sliced asparagus (1-inch pieces)

1 package (5 ounces) baby arugula (4 cups)

½ cup shaved Parmesan cheese

¼ cup extra virgin olive oil

2 tablespoons lemon juice

1 tablespoon orange juice

1 clove garlic, minced

½ teaspoon salt

½ teaspoon grated lemon peel

⅛ teaspoon black pepper

1. Place sun-dried tomatoes in small bowl; cover with 1 cup boiling water. Let stand 5 minutes; drain well.

2. Bring medium saucepan of salted water to a boil. Add asparagus; cook 1 minute or until crisp-tender. Rinse under cold running water to stop cooking.

3. Combine arugula, asparagus, sun-dried tomatoes and cheese in large bowl. Whisk oil, lemon juice, orange juice, garlic, salt, lemon peel and pepper in small bowl until well blended. Pour over salad; toss gently to coat.

CHEESY SPINACH CASSEROLE

MAKES 6 SERVINGS

1 pound baby spinach

4 slices bacon, chopped

1 small onion, chopped

1 cup sliced mushrooms

¼ cup chopped red bell pepper

3 cloves garlic, minced

1½ teaspoons minced canned chipotle peppers in adobo sauce

1 teaspoon seasoned salt

8 ounces pasteurized process cheese product, cut into pieces

½ (8-ounce) package cream cheese, cut into pieces

1 cup thawed frozen corn

½ cup (2 ounces) shredded Monterey Jack and Cheddar cheese blend

1. Preheat oven to 350°F. Spray 1-quart baking dish with nonstick cooking spray.

2. Heat large saucepan of water to a boil over high heat. Add spinach; cook 1 minute. Drain and transfer to bowl of ice water to stop cooking. Drain and squeeze spinach dry; set aside. Wipe out saucepan with paper towel.

3. Cook bacon in same saucepan over medium-high heat until almost crisp, stirring frequently. Drain off all but 1 tablespoon drippings. Add onion to saucepan; cook and stir 3 minutes or until softened. Add mushrooms and bell pepper; cook and stir 5 minutes or until vegetables are tender. Add garlic, chipotle and seasoned salt; cook and stir 1 minute.

4. Add process cheese and cream cheese to saucepan; cook over medium heat until melted, stirring frequently. Add spinach and corn; cook and stir 3 minutes. Transfer to prepared baking dish; sprinkle with shredded cheese.

5. Bake 20 to 25 minutes or until casserole is bubbly and cheese is melted. If desired, broil 1 to 2 minutes to brown top of casserole.

FARMERS' MARKET POTATO SALAD

MAKES 6 SERVINGS

Pickled Red Onions
(recipe follows)

2 cups cubed assorted
potatoes (purple, baby
red, Yukon Gold and/or
a combination)

1 cup fresh green beans,
cut into 1-inch pieces

2 tablespoons plain
Greek yogurt

2 tablespoons white
wine vinegar

2 tablespoons olive oil

1 tablespoon spicy mustard

1 teaspoon salt

1. Prepare Pickled Red Onions.

2. Bring large saucepan of lightly salted water to a boil. Add potatoes; cook 5 to 8 minutes or until fork-tender.* Add green beans during last 4 minutes of cooking time. Drain potatoes and green beans.

3. Whisk yogurt, vinegar, oil, mustard and salt in large bowl until smooth and well blended.

4. Add potatoes, green beans and pickled onions to dressing; toss gently to coat. Cover and refrigerate at least 1 hour before serving.

Some varieties of potatoes may take longer to cook than others. Remove individual potatoes to large bowl with slotted spoon when fork-tender.

PICKLED RED ONIONS: Combine ½ cup thinly sliced red onion, ¼ cup white wine vinegar, 2 tablespoons water, 1 teaspoon sugar and ½ teaspoon salt in large glass jar. Seal jar; shake well. Refrigerate at least 1 hour or up to 1 week.

BRUSSELS SPROUTS WITH HONEY BUTTER

MAKES 4 SERVINGS

6 slices thick-cut bacon, cut into ½-inch pieces

1½ pounds brussels sprouts (about 24 medium), halved

¼ teaspoon salt

¼ teaspoon black pepper

2 tablespoons butter, softened

2 tablespoons honey

1. Preheat oven to 375°F. Cook bacon in medium skillet until almost crisp. Drain on paper towel-lined plate; set aside. Reserve 1 tablespoon drippings for cooking brussels sprouts.

2. Place brussels sprouts on large baking sheet. Drizzle with reserved bacon drippings. Sprinkle with ¼ teaspoon salt and ¼ teaspoon pepper; toss to coat. Spread in single layer on baking sheet.

3. Roast 30 minutes or until brussels sprouts are browned and crispy, stirring once.

4. Meanwhile, combine butter and honey in medium bowl; mix well. Add hot roasted brussels sprouts; stir until completely coated. Stir in bacon; season with additional salt and pepper.

GARLIC KNOTS

MAKES 20 KNOTS

¾ cup warm water (105° to 115°F)

1 package (¼ ounce) active dry yeast

1 teaspoon sugar

2¼ cups all-purpose flour

2 tablespoons olive oil, divided

1½ teaspoons salt, divided

4 tablespoons (½ stick) butter, divided

1 tablespoon minced garlic

¼ teaspoon garlic powder

½ cup grated Parmesan cheese

2 tablespoons chopped fresh parsley

½ teaspoon dried oregano

1. Combine water, yeast and sugar in large bowl of electric stand mixer; stir to dissolve yeast. Let stand 5 minutes or until bubbly. Stir in flour, 1 tablespoon oil and 1 teaspoon salt; knead with dough hook at low speed 5 minutes or until dough is smooth and elastic. Shape dough into a ball. Place in large lightly greased bowl; turn to grease top. Cover and let rise 1 hour or until doubled in size.

2. Melt 2 tablespoons butter in small saucepan over low heat. Add remaining 1 tablespoon oil, ½ teaspoon salt, minced garlic and garlic powder; cook over very low heat 5 minutes. Pour into small bowl; set aside.

3. Preheat oven to 400°F. Line baking sheet with parchment paper.

4. Turn out dough onto lightly floured surface. Punch down dough; let stand 10 minutes. Roll out dough into 10×8-inch rectangle. Cut into 20 (2-inch) squares. Roll each piece into 8-inch rope; tie in a knot. Place knots on prepared baking sheet; brush with garlic mixture.

5. Bake 10 minutes or until knots are lightly browned. Meanwhile, melt remaining 2 tablespoons butter. Combine cheese, parsley and oregano in small bowl; mix well. Brush melted butter over baked knots; immediately sprinkle with cheese mixture. Cool slightly; serve warm.

TANGY RED CABBAGE WITH APPLES AND BACON

MAKES 4 SERVINGS

8 slices thick-cut bacon

1 large onion, sliced

½ small head red cabbage (about 1 pound), thinly sliced

1 tablespoon sugar

1 Granny Smith apple, peeled and sliced

2 tablespoons cider vinegar

½ teaspoon salt

¼ teaspoon black pepper

1. Cook bacon in large skillet over medium-high heat 6 to 8 minutes or until crisp, turning occasionally. Drain on paper towel-lined plate. Coarsely chop bacon.

2. Drain all but 2 tablespoons drippings from skillet. Add onion; cook and stir over medium-high heat 2 to 3 minutes or until onion begins to soften. Add cabbage and sugar; cook and stir 4 to 5 minutes or until cabbage wilts. Stir in apple; cook 3 minutes or until crisp-tender. Add vinegar; cook and stir 1 minute or until absorbed.

3. Stir in bacon, salt and pepper; cook 1 minute or until heated through. Serve warm or at room temperature.

HEARTY HASH BROWN CASSEROLE

MAKES ABOUT 16 SERVINGS

2 cups sour cream

2 cups (8 ounces) shredded Colby cheese, divided

1 can (10¾ ounces) cream of chicken soup

½ cup (1 stick) butter, melted

1 small onion, finely chopped

¾ teaspoon salt

½ teaspoon black pepper

1 package (30 ounces) frozen shredded hash brown potatoes, thawed

1. Preheat oven to 375°F. Spray 13×9-inch baking dish with nonstick cooking spray.

2. Combine sour cream, 1½ cups cheese, soup, butter, onion, salt and pepper in large bowl; mix well. Add potatoes; stir until well blended. Spread mixture in prepared baking dish. (Do not pack down.) Sprinkle with remaining ½ cup cheese.

3. Bake about 45 minutes or until cheese is melted and top of casserole is beginning to brown.

CREAMY COLESLAW

MAKES 8 SERVINGS

½ cup light mayonnaise

½ cup buttermilk

2 teaspoons sugar

1 teaspoon celery seed

1 teaspoon lime juice

½ teaspoon chili powder

3 cups shredded coleslaw mix

1 cup shredded carrots

¼ cup finely chopped red onion

1. Whisk mayonnaise, buttermilk, sugar, celery seed, lime juice and chili powder in large bowl until well blended.

2. Add coleslaw mix, carrots and onion; toss to coat. Cover and refrigerate at least 2 hours before serving.

ASPARAGUS WITH MUSTARD SAUCE

MAKES 6 SERVINGS

2 cups water

1½ pounds asparagus, trimmed

½ cup plain yogurt

2 tablespoons mayonnaise

1 tablespoon Dijon mustard

2 teaspoons lemon juice

½ teaspoon salt

Grated lemon peel (optional)

1. Bring water to a boil in large skillet over high heat. Add asparagus; return to a boil. Reduce heat; cover and cook 3 minutes or until crisp-tender. Drain.

2. Meanwhile, whisk yogurt, mayonnaise, mustard, lemon juice and salt in small bowl until well blended.

3. Place asparagus on serving platter; top with sauce. Garnish with lemon peel.

SMASHED POTATOES

MAKES 4 SERVINGS

4 medium russet potatoes (about 1½ pounds), peeled and cut into ¼-inch pieces

⅓ cup milk

2 tablespoons sour cream

1 tablespoon minced onion

½ teaspoon salt

¼ teaspoon black pepper

⅛ teaspoon garlic powder (optional)

Chopped fresh chives or French fried onions

1. Bring large saucepan of lightly salted water to a boil. Add potatoes; cook 15 to 20 minutes or until fork-tender. Drain and return to saucepan.

2. Slightly mash potatoes. Stir in milk, sour cream, onion, salt, pepper and garlic powder, if desired. Mash until desired texture is reached, leaving potatoes chunky. Cook over low heat 5 minutes or until heated through, stirring occasionally. Top with chives, if desired.

SKILLET MAC AND CHEESE

MAKES 6 SERVINGS

1 pound uncooked cavatappi or rotini pasta

8 ounces thick-cut bacon, cut into ½-inch pieces

¼ cup finely chopped onion

¼ cup all-purpose flour

3½ cups whole milk

1 cup (4 ounces) shredded white Cheddar cheese

1 cup (4 ounces) shredded fontina cheese

1 cup (4 ounces) shredded Gruyère cheese

¾ cup grated Parmesan cheese, divided

½ teaspoon salt

½ teaspoon dry mustard

¼ teaspoon ground red pepper

¼ teaspoon black pepper

¼ cup panko bread crumbs

1. Preheat oven to 400°F. Cook pasta according to package directions until al dente; drain.

2. Meanwhile, cook bacon in large cast iron skillet until crisp; drain on paper towel-lined plate. Pour drippings into glass measuring cup, leaving thin coating on surface of skillet.

3. Heat 4 tablespoons drippings in large saucepan over medium-high heat. Add onion; cook and stir 3 minutes or until translucent. Add flour; cook and stir 5 minutes. Slowly add milk over medium-low heat, stirring constantly. Stir in Cheddar, fontina, Gruyère, ½ cup Parmesan, salt, mustard, red pepper and black pepper until smooth and well blended. Add cooked pasta; stir gently until coated. Stir in bacon. Spread mixture in cast iron skillet.

4. Combine panko and remaining ¼ cup Parmesan in small bowl; sprinkle over pasta. Bake 30 minutes or until top is golden brown.

DESSERTS

SWEET POTATO PECAN PIE

MAKES 8 SERVINGS

1 sweet potato
(about 1 pound)

3 eggs, divided

8 tablespoons granulated
sugar, divided

8 tablespoons packed
brown sugar, divided

2 tablespoons butter, melted,
divided

½ teaspoon ground cinnamon

½ teaspoon salt, divided

1 frozen 9-inch deep-dish
pie crust

½ cup dark corn syrup

1½ teaspoons vanilla

1½ teaspoons lemon juice

1 cup pecan halves

Vanilla ice cream (optional)

1. Preheat oven to 350°F. Prick sweet potato all over with fork. Bake 1 hour or until fork-tender; let stand until cool enough to handle. Peel sweet potato; place in bowl of electric stand mixer. *Reduce oven temperature to 300°F.*

2. Add 1 egg, 2 tablespoons granulated sugar, 2 tablespoons brown sugar, 1 tablespoon butter, cinnamon and ¼ teaspoon salt to bowl with sweet potato; beat at medium speed 5 minutes or until smooth and fluffy. Spread mixture in frozen crust; place in refrigerator.

3. Combine corn syrup, remaining 6 tablespoons granulated sugar, 6 tablespoons brown sugar, 1 tablespoon butter, vanilla, lemon juice and remaining ¼ teaspoon salt in clean mixer bowl; beat at medium speed 5 minutes. Add remaining 2 eggs; beat 5 minutes. Place crust on baking sheet. Spread pecans over sweet potato filling; pour corn syrup mixture evenly over pecans.

4. Bake 1 hour or until center is set and top is deep golden brown. Cool completely. Serve with ice cream, if desired.

BLUEBERRY APPLE SKILLET CRUMBLE

MAKES 6 TO 8 SERVINGS

TOPPING

- 1 cup all-purpose flour
- ⅔ cup sugar
- ¼ teaspoon salt
- ¼ teaspoon ground cinnamon
- ½ cup (1 stick) butter, cut into small pieces

FRUIT

- 2 packages (12 ounces each) frozen blueberries (do not thaw)
- 4 Granny Smith apples, peeled and thinly sliced
- 3 tablespoons all-purpose flour
- 3 tablespoons sugar
- 1 teaspoon lemon juice
- ¼ teaspoon ground cinnamon

1. Preheat oven to 350°F.

2. For topping, combine 1 cup flour, ⅔ cup sugar, salt and ¼ teaspoon cinnamon in medium bowl; mix well. Add butter; mix with fingertips until large clumps form.

3. For fruit, combine blueberries, apples, 3 tablespoons flour, 3 tablespoons sugar, lemon juice and ¼ teaspoon cinnamon in large bowl; mix well. Pour into large cast iron skillet. Spread topping over fruit. Place skillet on baking sheet.

4. Bake 55 to 60 minutes or until fruit mixture is bubbling around edges and topping is crisp and beginning to brown.

CARROT CAKE

MAKES 8 TO 10 SERVINGS

CAKE

- 2 cups all-purpose flour
- 2 teaspoons baking soda
- 2 teaspoons ground cinnamon
- 1 teaspoon salt
- 4 eggs
- 2¼ cups granulated sugar
- 1 cup vegetable oil
- 1 cup buttermilk
- 1 tablespoon vanilla
- 3 medium carrots, shredded (3 cups)
- 3 cups walnuts, chopped and toasted, divided
- 1 cup shredded coconut
- 1 can (8 ounces) crushed pineapple

FROSTING

- 2 packages (8 ounces each) cream cheese, softened
- 1 cup (2 sticks) butter, softened

  Pinch of salt
- 3 cups powdered sugar
- 1 tablespoon orange juice
- 2 teaspoons grated orange peel
- 1 teaspoon vanilla

1. Preheat oven to 350°F. Spray two 9-inch round cake pans with nonstick cooking spray. Line bottoms of pans with parchment paper; spray with cooking spray.

2. For cake, combine flour, baking soda, cinnamon and 1 teaspoon salt in medium bowl; mix well. Whisk eggs in large bowl until blended. Add granulated sugar, oil, buttermilk and 1 tablespoon vanilla; whisk until well blended. Add flour mixture; stir until well blended. Add carrots, 1 cup walnuts, coconut and pineapple; stir just until blended. Pour batter into prepared pans.

3. Bake 25 to 30 minutes or until toothpick inserted into centers comes out clean. Cool in pans 10 minutes; remove to wire racks to cool completely.

4. For frosting, beat cream cheese, butter and pinch of salt in large bowl with electric mixer at medium speed 3 minutes or until creamy. Add powdered sugar, orange juice, orange peel and 1 teaspoon vanilla; beat at low speed until blended. Beat at medium speed 2 minutes or until frosting is smooth.

5. Place one cake layer on serving plate. Top with 2 cups frosting; spread evenly. Top with second cake layer; frost top and side of cake with remaining frosting. Press 1³⁄₄ cups walnuts onto side of cake. Sprinkle remaining ¹⁄₄ cup walnuts over top of cake.

CHOCOLATE WHOOPIE PIES

MAKES ABOUT 2 DOZEN SANDWICH COOKIES

1¾ cups all-purpose flour
½ cup unsweetened Dutch process cocoa powder
¾ teaspoon baking powder
½ teaspoon baking soda
½ teaspoon salt
1 cup packed brown sugar

1 cup (2 sticks) butter, softened, divided
1 egg
1½ teaspoons vanilla, divided
1 cup milk
1 cup marshmallow creme
1 cup powdered sugar

1. Preheat oven to 350°F. Line cookie sheets with parchment paper.

2. Sift flour, cocoa, baking powder, baking soda and salt into medium bowl. Beat brown sugar and ½ cup butter in large bowl with electric mixer at medium-high speed about 3 minutes or until light and fluffy. Beat in egg and 1 teaspoon vanilla until well blended. Alternately add flour mixture and milk, beating at low speed after each addition until smooth and well blended. Drop dough by heaping teaspoonfuls 2 inches apart onto prepared cookie sheets.

3. Bake 8 to 10 minutes or until cookies are puffed and tops spring back when lightly touched. Cool on cookie sheets 10 minutes; remove to wire racks to cool completely.

4. Meanwhile, prepare filling. Beat remaining ½ cup butter, ½ teaspoon vanilla, marshmallow creme and powdered sugar in large bowl with electric mixer at high speed 2 minutes or until light and fluffy.

5. Pipe or spread heaping teaspoon filling onto flat side of half of cookies; top with remaining cookies.

WARM APPLE CROSTATA
MAKES 4 TARTS (4 TO 8 SERVINGS)

1¾ cups all-purpose flour

⅓ cup granulated sugar

½ teaspoon plus ⅛ teaspoon salt, divided

¾ cup (1½ sticks) cold butter, cut into small pieces

3 tablespoons ice water

2 teaspoons vanilla

8 Pink Lady or Honeycrisp apples (about 1½ pounds), peeled and cut into ¼-inch slices

¼ cup packed brown sugar

1 tablespoon lemon juice

1 teaspoon ground cinnamon

⅛ teaspoon ground nutmeg

4 teaspoons butter, cut into very small pieces

1 egg, beaten

1 to 2 teaspoons coarse sugar

Vanilla ice cream

Caramel sauce or ice cream topping

1. Combine flour, granulated sugar and ½ teaspoon salt in food processor; process 5 seconds. Add ¾ cup butter; process about 10 seconds or until mixture resembles coarse crumbs.

2. Combine ice water and vanilla in small bowl. With motor running, pour mixture through feed tube; process 12 seconds or until dough begins to come together. Shape dough into a disc; wrap in plastic wrap and refrigerate 30 minutes.

3. Meanwhile, combine apples, brown sugar, lemon juice, cinnamon, nutmeg and remaining ⅛ teaspoon salt in large bowl; toss to coat. Preheat oven to 400°F.

4. Line two baking sheets with parchment paper. Cut dough into four pieces; roll out each piece into 7-inch circle on floured surface. Place on prepared baking sheets; mound apples in center of dough circles (about 1 cup apples for each crostata). Fold or roll up edges of dough towards center to create rim of crostata. Dot apples with remaining 4 teaspoons butter. Brush dough with egg; sprinkle dough and apples with coarse sugar.

5. Bake about 20 minutes or until apples are tender and crust is golden brown. Serve warm topped with ice cream and caramel sauce.

CHOCOLATE PECAN BARS

MAKES 2 DOZEN BARS

CRUST

1⅓ cups all-purpose flour

½ cup (1 stick) butter, softened

¼ cup packed brown sugar

½ teaspoon salt

TOPPING

¾ cup light corn syrup

3 eggs, lightly beaten

2 tablespoons butter, melted and cooled

½ teaspoon vanilla

½ teaspoon almond extract

¾ cup milk chocolate chips

¾ cup semisweet chocolate chips

¾ cup chopped pecans, toasted*

¾ cup granulated sugar

To toast pecans, spread on baking sheet. Bake in preheated 350°F oven 5 to 7 minutes or until lightly browned and fragrant, stirring frequently.

1. Preheat oven to 350°F. Spray 13×9-inch baking pan with nonstick cooking spray.

2. For crust, combine flour, ½ cup butter, brown sugar and salt in medium bowl; mix with fork until crumbly. Press into bottom of prepared baking pan. Bake 12 to 15 minutes or until lightly browned. Let stand 10 minutes.

3. Meanwhile, for topping, combine corn syrup, eggs, 2 tablespoons butter, vanilla and almond extract in large bowl; stir with fork until combined (do not beat). Fold in chocolate chips, pecans and granulated sugar until blended. Pour over baked crust.

4. Bake 25 to 30 minutes or until toothpick inserted into center comes out clean. Cool completely in pan on wire rack.

GLAZED APPLESAUCE SPICE CAKE
MAKES 12 SERVINGS

1 cup packed brown sugar

¾ cup (1½ sticks) butter, softened

3 eggs

1½ teaspoons vanilla

2¼ cups all-purpose flour

2 teaspoons baking soda

2 teaspoons ground cinnamon

¾ teaspoon ground nutmeg

½ teaspoon ground ginger

¼ teaspoon salt

1½ cups unsweetened applesauce

½ cup milk

⅔ cup chopped walnuts

⅔ cup butterscotch chips

Apple Glaze (recipe follows)

1. Preheat oven to 350°F. Grease and flour 12-cup bundt pan or 10-inch tube pan.

2. Beat brown sugar and butter in large bowl with electric mixer at medium speed until light and fluffy. Beat in eggs and vanilla until well blended.

3. Combine flour, baking soda, cinnamon, nutmeg, ginger and salt in medium bowl. Add to butter mixture alternately with applesauce and milk, beginning and ending with flour mixture, beating well after each addition. Stir in walnuts and butterscotch chips. Pour batter into prepared pan.

4. Bake 45 to 50 minutes or until toothpick inserted near center comes out clean. Cool in pan 15 minutes; invert onto wire rack to cool completely.

5. Prepare Apple Glaze; spoon over cake.

APPLE GLAZE: Place 1 cup sifted powdered sugar in small bowl. Whisk in 2 to 3 tablespoons apple juice concentrate to make stiff glaze.

PLUM RHUBARB CRISP

MAKES 6 TO 8 SERVINGS

1½ pounds plums, each pitted and cut into 8 wedges (4 cups)

1½ pounds rhubarb, cut into ½-inch pieces (5 cups)

1 cup granulated sugar

1 teaspoon finely grated fresh ginger

¼ teaspoon ground nutmeg

3 tablespoons cornstarch

¾ cup old-fashioned oats

½ cup all-purpose flour

½ cup packed brown sugar

½ cup sliced almonds, toasted*

¼ teaspoon salt

½ cup (1 stick) cold butter, cut into small pieces

To toast almonds, spread in single layer on ungreased baking sheet. Bake in preheated 350°F oven 5 minutes or until golden brown, stirring frequently.

1. Combine plums, rhubarb, granulated sugar, ginger and nutmeg in large bowl; toss to coat. Cover and let stand at room temperature 2 hours.

2. Preheat oven to 375°F. Spray 9-inch round or square baking dish with nonstick cooking spray. Line baking sheet with foil.

3. Pour juices from fruit mixture into small saucepan; bring to a boil over medium-high heat. Cook about 12 minutes or until liquid is reduced to syrupy consistency, stirring occasionally.* Stir in cornstarch until well blended. Stir mixture into bowl with fruit; pour into prepared baking dish.

4. Combine oats, flour, brown sugar, almonds and salt in medium bowl; mix well. Add butter; mix with fingertips until butter is evenly distributed and mixture is clumpy. Sprinkle evenly over fruit mixture. Place baking dish on prepared baking sheet.

5. Bake about 50 minutes or until filling is bubbly and topping is golden brown. Cool 1 hour before serving.

If fruit is not juicy after 2 hours, liquid will take less time to reduce and require less cornstarch to thicken.

LEMON MERINGUE PIE

MAKES 8 SERVINGS

1 (9-inch) frozen pie crust

4 eggs, at room temperature

3 tablespoons lemon juice

2 tablespoons butter, melted

2 teaspoons grated lemon peel

3 drops yellow food coloring (optional)

⅔ cup sugar, divided

1 cup cold water

¼ cup cornstarch

⅛ teaspoon salt

¼ teaspoon vanilla

1. Preheat oven to 425°F. Bake pie crust according to package directions.

2. Separate eggs; discard 2 egg yolks. Combine lemon juice, butter, lemon peel and food coloring, if desired, in small bowl; mix well.

3. Reserve 2 tablespoons sugar. Combine water, remaining sugar, cornstarch and salt in medium saucepan; whisk until smooth. Bring to a boil over medium-high heat, whisking constantly. Reduce heat to medium; boil 1 minute, whisking constantly. Remove from heat.

4. Stir ¼ cup hot sugar mixture into egg yolks in small bowl until well blended, whisking constantly. Slowly whisk egg yolk mixture back into hot sugar mixture. Cook over medium heat 3 minutes, whisking constantly. Remove from heat; stir in lemon juice mixture until well blended. Pour into baked pie crust.

5. Beat egg whites in large bowl with electric mixer at high speed until soft peaks form. Gradually beat in reserved 2 tablespoons sugar and vanilla; beat until stiff peaks form. Spread meringue over pie filling with rubber spatula, making sure meringue completely covers filling and touches edge of pie crust.

6. Bake 5 to 10 minutes or until meringue is lightly browned. Cool completely on wire rack. Cover with plastic wrap; refrigerate 8 hours or overnight until filling is firm and pie is thoroughly chilled.

APRICOT OATMEAL BARS

MAKES 9 SERVINGS

1½ cups old-fashioned oats

1¼ cups all-purpose flour

½ cup packed brown sugar

1 teaspoon ground ginger, divided

½ teaspoon salt

½ teaspoon baking soda

½ teaspoon ground cinnamon

¾ cup (1½ sticks) butter, melted

1¼ cups apricot preserves

1. Preheat oven to 350°F. Line 8-inch square baking pan with foil.

2. Combine oats, flour, brown sugar, ½ teaspoon ginger, salt, baking soda and cinnamon in large bowl; mix well. Add butter; stir just until moistened and crumbly. Reserve 1½ cups oat mixture for topping; press remaining oat mixture evenly onto bottom of prepared pan.

3. Combine preserves and remaining ½ teaspoon ginger in small bowl; mix well. Spread evenly over crust; sprinkle with reserved oat mixture.

4. Bake 30 minutes or until golden brown. Cool completely in pan on wire rack.

CHOCOLATE BANANA PEANUT BUTTER POKE CAKE

MAKES 12 TO 15 SERVINGS

1 package (about 15 ounces) chocolate cake mix, plus ingredients to prepare mix

½ cup (1 stick) butter, softened

½ cup peanut butter (not natural)

4 to 5 teaspoons milk

1 to 2 cups powdered sugar

1 package (4-serving size) banana cream instant pudding and pie filling mix, plus ingredients to prepare mix

1. Prepare and bake cake mix according to package directions for 13×9-inch pan. Cool completely in pan on wire rack.

2. Beat butter in medium bowl with electric mixer at medium speed until light and fluffy. Add peanut butter and milk; beat 2 minutes or until fluffy. Gradually beat in powdered sugar, ¼ cup at a time, until frosting reaches spreadable consistency.

3. Poke holes in cake at ½-inch intervals with wooden skewer. Prepare pudding mix according to package directions. Pour pudding over cake; top with peanut butter frosting. Refrigerate 2 to 3 hours or until firm.

STRAWBERRY RHUBARB PIE

MAKES 8 SERVINGS

Double-Crust Pie Pastry (recipe follows)

1½ cups granulated sugar

½ cup cornstarch

2 tablespoons quick-cooking tapioca

1 tablespoon grated lemon peel

¼ teaspoon ground allspice

4 cups sliced rhubarb (1-inch pieces)

3 cups sliced fresh strawberries

1 egg, lightly beaten

Coarse sugar (optional)

1. Prepare Double-Crust Pie Pastry.

2. Preheat oven to 425°F. Roll out one pastry disc into 11-inch circle on floured surface. Line 9-inch pie plate with pastry.

3. Combine granulated sugar, cornstarch, tapioca, lemon peel and allspice in large bowl; mix well. Add rhubarb and strawberries; toss to coat. Pour into crust.

4. Roll out remaining pastry disc into 10-inch circle; cut into ½-inch-wide strips. Arrange in lattice design over fruit; seal and flute edge. Brush pastry with beaten egg. Sprinkle with coarse sugar, if desired.

5. Bake 50 minutes or until filling is thick and bubbly and crust is golden brown. Cool on wire rack. Serve warm or at room temperature.

DOUBLE-CRUST PIE PASTRY: Combine 2½ cups all-purpose flour, 1 teaspoon salt and 1 teaspoon sugar in large bowl; mix well. Cut in 1 cup (2 sticks) cubed unsalted butter with pastry blender or two knives until mixture resembles coarse crumbs. Drizzle ⅓ cup cold water over flour mixture, 2 tablespoons at a time, stirring just until dough comes together. Divide dough in half. Shape each half into a disc; wrap in plastic wrap. Refrigerate 30 minutes.

CREAMY LEMON CHEESECAKE

MAKES 12 SERVINGS

9 graham crackers, crushed into crumbs

⅓ cup ground blanched almonds

6 tablespoons (¾ stick) butter, melted

¾ cup plus 2 tablespoons sugar, divided

3 packages (8 ounces each) cream cheese, softened

1 container (15 ounces) ricotta cheese

4 eggs, beaten

2 tablespoons finely grated lemon peel

1 teaspoon lemon extract

1 teaspoon vanilla

1. Preheat oven to 375°F.

2. Combine graham cracker crumbs, almonds, butter and 2 tablespoons sugar in medium bowl; mix well. Press evenly onto bottom and ½ inch up side of 9-inch springform pan. Bake 5 minutes. Remove to wire rack to cool. *Reduce oven temperature to 325°F.*

3. Beat cream cheese, ricotta, eggs, remaining ¾ cup sugar, lemon peel, lemon extract and vanilla in large bowl with electric mixer at low speed until blended. Beat at high speed 4 to 5 minutes until smooth and creamy. Pour into crust.

4. Bake 1 hour and 10 minutes or just until set in center. *Do not overbake.* Remove to wire rack to cool to room temperature. Cover and refrigerate 4 hours or overnight.

SNICKERDOODLES

MAKES ABOUT 3 DOZEN COOKIES

¾ cup plus 2 tablespoons sugar, divided

2 teaspoons ground cinnamon, divided

1⅓ cups all-purpose flour

1 teaspoon cream of tartar

½ teaspoon baking soda

½ teaspoon salt

½ cup (1 stick) butter, softened

1 egg

1. Preheat oven to 375°F. Line cookie sheets with parchment paper.

2. Combine 2 tablespoons sugar and 1 teaspoon cinnamon in small bowl; set aside. Combine flour, remaining 1 teaspoon cinnamon, cream of tartar, baking soda and salt in medium bowl; mix well.

3. Beat remaining ¾ cup sugar and butter in large bowl with electric mixer at medium speed until creamy. Beat in egg until well blended. Gradually add flour mixture, beating at low speed until stiff dough forms. Roll dough into 1-inch balls; roll in cinnamon-sugar mixture. Place on prepared cookie sheets.

4. Bake 10 minutes or just until set. *Do not overbake*. Remove to wire racks to cool completely.

OLD-FASHIONED DEVIL'S FOOD CAKE

MAKES 12 SERVINGS

6 tablespoons (¾ stick) butter, softened

1½ cups granulated sugar

3 eggs

1½ teaspoons vanilla

2 cups cake flour

½ cup unsweetened cocoa powder

2 teaspoons baking powder

½ teaspoon baking soda

½ teaspoon salt

1 cup buttermilk*

Creamy Chocolate Frosting (recipe follows)

*If buttermilk is unavailable, substitute 1 tablespoon vinegar or lemon juice and enough milk to equal 1 cup. Stir; let stand 5 minutes.

1. Preheat oven to 350°F. Grease and flour three 8-inch round cake pans.

2. Beat butter and granulated sugar in large bowl with electric mixer at medium speed until fluffy. Beat in eggs and vanilla.

3. Combine flour, cocoa, baking powder, baking soda and salt in medium bowl; mix well. Add to butter mixture alternately with buttermilk, beating well after each addition. Pour batter evenly into prepared pans.

4. Bake 25 to 30 minutes or until toothpick inserted into centers comes out clean. Cool in pans 10 minutes; remove to wire racks to cool completely.

5. Meanwhile, prepare Creamy Chocolate Frosting. Place one cake layer on serving plate; spread with frosting. Repeat with remaining two cake layers and frosting. Frost side and top of cake.

CREAMY CHOCOLATE FROSTING: Beat 6 tablespoons (¾ stick) softened butter in large bowl with electric mixer at medium speed until creamy. Gradually add 5 cups powdered sugar and cocoa, beating until smooth. Add 6 tablespoons milk and 1 teaspoon vanilla; beat until desired consistency is reached.

INDEX

INDEX

INDEX

METRIC CONVERSION CHART

VOLUME MEASUREMENTS (dry)

1/8 teaspoon = 0.5 mL
1/4 teaspoon = 1 mL
1/2 teaspoon = 2 mL
3/4 teaspoon = 4 mL
1 teaspoon = 5 mL
1 tablespoon = 15 mL
2 tablespoons = 30 mL
1/4 cup = 60 mL
1/3 cup = 75 mL
1/2 cup = 125 mL
2/3 cup = 150 mL
3/4 cup = 175 mL
1 cup = 250 mL
2 cups = 1 pint = 500 mL
3 cups = 750 mL
4 cups = 1 quart = 1 L

VOLUME MEASUREMENTS (fluid)

1 fluid ounce (2 tablespoons) = 30 mL
4 fluid ounces (1/2 cup) = 125 mL
8 fluid ounces (1 cup) = 250 mL
12 fluid ounces (1 1/2 cups) = 375 mL
16 fluid ounces (2 cups) = 500 mL

WEIGHTS (mass)

1/2 ounce = 15 g
1 ounce = 30 g
3 ounces = 90 g
4 ounces = 120 g
8 ounces = 225 g
10 ounces = 285 g
12 ounces = 360 g
16 ounces = 1 pound = 450 g

DIMENSIONS

1/16 inch = 2 mm
1/8 inch = 3 mm
1/4 inch = 6 mm
1/2 inch = 1.5 cm
3/4 inch = 2 cm
1 inch = 2.5 cm

OVEN TEMPERATURES

250°F = 120°C
275°F = 140°C
300°F = 150°C
325°F = 160°C
350°F = 180°C
375°F = 190°C
400°F = 200°C
425°F = 220°C
450°F = 230°C

BAKING PAN SIZES

Utensil	Size in Inches/Quarts	Metric Volume	Size in Centimeters
Baking or Cake Pan (square or rectangular)	8×8×2	2 L	20×20×5
	9×9×2	2.5 L	23×23×5
	12×8×2	3 L	30×20×5
	13×9×2	3.5 L	33×23×5
Loaf Pan	8×4×3	1.5 L	20×10×7
	9×5×3	2 L	23×13×7
Round Layer Cake Pan	8×1½	1.2 L	20×4
	9×1½	1.5 L	23×4
Pie Plate	8×1¼	750 mL	20×3
	9×1¼	1 L	23×3
Baking Dish or Casserole	1 quart	1 L	—
	1½ quart	1.5 L	—
	2 quart	2 L	—